IN THE STREETZ 4

Weather The Storm

TRON HILL

URBAN AINT DEAD

URBAN AINT DEAD
P.O Box 448
Maybrook, NY 12543

All rights reserved. Published by URBAN AINT DEAD Publications.

Cover Design: P Wise / The Wise Services

Edited By: Shawna Brim / Ladies of Lit

URBAN AINT DEAD and coinciding logo(s) are registered properties.

Contact Publisher at www.urbanaintdead.com

Email: urbanaintdead@gmail.com

Print ISBN: 979-8-9908882-1-0

SOUNDTRACKS

Scan the QR Code below to listen to the Soundtracks/Singles of some of your favorite U.A.D titles:

Don't have Spotify or Apple Music?
No Sweat!
Visit your choice streaming platform and search URBAN AINT DEAD.

Currently on lock serving a bid?
JPay, iHeartRadio, WHATEVER!
We got you covered.
Simply log into your facility's kiosk or tablet, go to music and search
URBAN AINT DEAD.

URBAN AINT DEAD

Like & Follow us on social media:

FB - URBAN AINT DEAD

IG: @urbanaintdead

Tik Tok - @urbanaintdead

Submission Guidelines

Submit the first three chapters of your completed manuscript to urbanaintdead@gmail.com, subject line: Your book's title. The manuscript must be in a .doc file and sent as an attachment. The document should be in Times New Roman, double-spaced, and in size 12 font. Also, provide your synopsis and full contact information. If sending multiple submissions, they must each be in a separate email. Have a story but no way to submit it electronically? You can still submit to URBAN AINT DEAD. Send in the first three chapters, written or typed, of your completed manuscript to:

URBAN AINT DEAD
P.O Box 448
Maybrook, NY 12543

DO NOT send original manuscript. Must be a duplicate.
Provide your synopsis and a cover letter containing your full contact information.
Thanks for considering URBAN AINT DEAD.

CHAPTER 1

ASHER TOOK a second drag of the Cuban cigar while relaxing on the Italian chair which possessed the appearance of belonging to royalty. Letting the smoke swirl from his mouth, he smirked amusingly at his guest, who stood on the opposite side of his beautiful mahogany desk. Before now, he'd only met the man once on the terms of him being introduced through a third party. And that had been nothing more than a simple nod of the head.

Asher wasn't what you'd call the *sociable* type. The only time he felt the urge to be was when business was in the process of being conducted. Which, for the guest's sake, needed to be the reason for the unexpected visit. Usually prior to sit downs, visitors were to make appointments where upon they'd be given a set time and place to handle the matter. However, this particular guest had barged into his office space — unannounced — carrying a large gym bag that apparently was occupied with something of weight.

The intruder must have clearly understood what the consequences of his trespassing would be because as soon as he was directly in front of him, he quickly uttered something that would have caught anybody's attention. "I got a lot of money and a proposition." Though his words hadn't stopped the instant drawing of the weapons by his two henchmen, they did however penetrate the ears of the one who'd been the direct controller of the trigger fingers on those weapons.

Asher took a few moments to study the man's face closely. If only he could see beyond those calculating eyes… Signaling to his guest to sit, Asher pulled on the cigar, wondering exactly how much money the individual had brought. Secondly, he needed to know what exactly the basis was for this so-called proposition. Dumping the ashes, he leaned forward in his chair. Sliding the ashtray directly between them, Asher asked with a nod toward the gym bag, "How much money?"

"Over three hundred thousand." The sound of his voice made it quite obvious that he prided himself on it.

Asher smiled then looked at his henchman to the right of the visitor. He knew from its size that even if it wasn't the number the man had uttered, it probably was still very, very close to that amount, though he was a little confused as to why he, out of all the people in the world, would walk into this domain with it. Evidently, the guy was very unaware of the predicament he'd put his money — and his life — in. He could easily lose both with a simple flick of the finger.

Squatting, the henchman hastily unzipped the bag. Asher closely watched the body language of his comrade from the other side of the desk. The man's eyes bulged as a sharp whistle came from his lips after he peered down into it. The shock-stricken face glanced up at the guest, who paid him no mind. His eyes remained sternly fixed on the henchman's boss. Lifting the duffle, he peeled the slit for the eyes of his chief.

Instantaneously, Asher pointed toward the desk. He wanted a better look at it. The henchman began to grip what he could with one hand and placed it on the desk.

This will take all day. Asher waved his hand, quickly pushing the ashtray from the center. His mouth watered at the sight of the tumbling stacks of cash. "It looks about right." Asher admired the beautiful pile before him. Nothing aroused him more than money. He could get off just by staring at it. His pulse quickened; he needed another pull from the cigar. Exhaling, he flipped one of the stacks in his hand. "And what exactly is this *proposition* you speak of?" He was very curious now.

The visitor smiled a few seconds. He was choosing the best way to put his next words. "I want in."

Immediately snatching the Cuban from his lips, Asher gave this little man an awkward look. He didn't know whether to be partly stunned or amused by the man's blatant audacity. Quickly tossing the money back to the pile and snubbing out the cigar's cherry, he moved around the desk. Asher pushed all the money to the side and tugged his slacks slightly upward before taking a seat directly in front of his out of line visitor.

"Let me understand this. You barge into my office, unannounced, with this money," he said, swinging his arm over it, "money that could possibly be counterfeit or worse, marked. But let's say it's neither and that it's all legit, all the way down to the single cent. What in the hell would make you think that this money could buy you a ticket *in*? When…" Asher paused to clear his throat.

"When you first strolled in without an invitation, I said to myself that this person has to be one of two things. One being that you are a person with something of the utmost urgency to bring to my attention. Or two being that you had to be a person with the nuts of a bull and the fucking brains of a damn turtle. But quickly, you say that you have *hundreds* of thousands and a simple proposition." He laughed, looking at both of his henchmen before straightening his tie. The brief occasion had become something quite comical.

"When I hear the word, *proposition,* I think of deals. Two or more transactions of some sort. You know, like *quid pro quo,* something reasonable exchanged for something reasonable. Like every other motherfucker that walks into this building expects!" he said intensely, lifting his eyes toward the ceiling. Then, he continued. "I don't even know your fucking name. But here you sit with your proposition being that you want in? Seriously, are you kidding me right now? Does this supposed to be a scene from one of those fucking Black novels?"

Releasing a mocking chuckle, Asher rubbed his silky hair backwards. He began to gesture with his hand as if he was about to say something else. But nothing came from his mouth. Closing his eyes, he took a deep breath while calmly resting his intertwined fingers on his thigh. Fully composed, he allowed his mischievous smirk to appear again.

"I think that you should give me a very convincing reason why I shouldn't have Aldo here," he nodded at the other henchman who was behind the visitor, the same one that had begun twisting a silencer onto the barrel on his weapon, "to do away with every part of you. And just to sum it all up right now, whether you die today or not, I'm keeping your money as a token of your deepest apologies for the bold visit and the stupid insult." Asher's face suddenly flushed red after getting the visitor's unfearful smile.

Of course, he could easily have the gleeful face distorted into something along the lines of pure agony and torment. But this was a place of business where the intelligent came to transact and trade in amounts that would make the visitor's luggage resemble that of a weekly nine to five paycheck. For the time being, which he determined would be very short, he'd play it cool. However, if the guy's next sentences lacked any real value, or didn't make actual sense, he'd quickly be taken care of right here, in this office. Then, his body would be discarded for his very fatal mistake.

The visitor's eyes became intense. "Because I know where Enzo's treasure is…"

Instantly, Asher's body became stiff as a tree. Memories from a past event flooded back into his mind. Enzo's treasure was in every sense a treasure. Yet, it was a treasure which consisted of a specific set of things which belonged to a particular somebody of importance — somebody who was the one to coin it *Enzo's Treasure*. Everyone who had heard about the situation knew that the christening had been out of pure mockery. The treasure itself had nothing to do with Enzo until he — somehow — manufactured a scheme into a reality, a reality which became the sole cause for the treasure being stolen and his very own life being taken along with it.

Asher couldn't remember how many times he had cursed his deceased little cousin for being so stupid, involving himself with the likes of people who he'd eventually warned him about — the same people who he himself had introduced Enzo to when he discreetly mentioned the jewels and his feelings toward attaining them. What a bad decision it turned out to be and a revelation Asher was determined to go to the grave with. Though that was only *his* determination. There existed four other individuals who knew as well. But his breathing body was enough proof that none of them had related the old introduction to anyone.

What good would it do for them at this point? He'd asked himself. The situation had occurred almost two years ago and the connection almost three. There existed nothing for them to gain by revealing it. The decision about their fates had been made, something he could never come to terms with.

Yes, Enzo had been disloyal and had made the naïve mistake of being blinded by greed. They were simple actions that a simple child would make, which Enzo was mentally. But he lost his life upon seeing an opportunity, something the elders in their family had taught them to do and take advantage of. So, why couldn't — or wouldn't — his uncle see it for what it was? See that Enzo stupidly thought he was taking advantage of an opportunity which he'd been manipulated into believing that he had a birthright to? Hadn't Uncle rose through the ranks of the family along the lines of a similar act? And above all, Enzo had been killed due to these people's treacherous natures, so why were their lives spared?

Asher couldn't remember how long it had been since he had these thoughts and questions. The *situation* — and everything that was attached to it — he'd put at a very long distance because there was nothing to gain from it. Only something to lose. And after all this time had passed, he had avoided losing it. Now here sat an unknown character, bringing it back into his life — a person he would have never expected to have knowledge of Enzo's existence, let alone the treasure and obviously the connection between everyone involved.

Without hesitation, Asher signaled for the silenced pistol. Gripping the weapon, he snatched the slide backwards, making sure one was in the chamber. "Out!!!" he growled at his henchmen, keeping his focus on the irritating individual in front of him. Upon hearing the latch click, Asher swiftly moved into position, placing the tip of the silencer against the flesh between the visitor's eyes. "What the fuck do you know about Enzo's treasure?" he snarled menacingly.

The visitor didn't seem a bit fazed nor intimidated by the action. His smile only broadened. "I know that the money was 4.6 million, but…" His words trailed off. He began to rub his hands together, preparing himself to expose exactly to what extent his knowledge went. "But the diamonds alone are more than fifty mill. And let's not forget the people who took it and *all* the people who are desperately trying to get their hands on them."

CHAPTER 2

AFTER PICKING up the artillery from Tweety, Ace paid a visit to Sassy's grave. This was something he always did when the burdens of reality had overwhelmed him physically and mentally. It had become his thinking place, a place he'd get the best consultation from. It was the only spot his thoughts were capable of reasoning with each other, something in much need at the current moment. So much was happening so fast that he had the slightest clue as where to start.

Dre had died, creating a new personal beef with Keith, who he felt was responsible for his protégé's early demise. Ace would have to move meticulously on him though. Keith had more goons on his side and a viciousness which matched his very own.

Then there was Stacey, his new top priority. She had played a major role in the situation that led to Sassy's death. They had negotiated a deal, and he had reneged on it. But the Feds had a million ways to deal with him. Instead, they chose to act out their sour intentions on the pregnant woman he loved more than life itself. They chose to take his love.

Now, he would force Stacey to disclose everyone who had participated in the kidnapping and her relationship with Paul. He cared little if she was unwilling; he'd force her to cough up everything she knew. Then, he'd allow her to make peace with God.

Ace smiled at the thought of the reunion. It was as if destiny had finally chosen a side — his side. After all the terrible nights, haunted by regret and fury, revenge was finally within his grasp. All the sleepless hours spent blaming himself, torturing his soul with thoughts of the endless games of survival — everything had led to this moment. Now, the tide was turning, and he could feel the shift in his favor. Soon, those who had wronged him would know the full extent of his wrath.

Out of all the latest events to take place, this particular one had been the wildest and most unforeseeable of them all. He had fallen in love with Ariel. Who would have thought there'd be a day when his heart would let another woman in, let another female fill Sassy's place? The feeling was bittersweet. He felt like it was a betrayal to the one who had his heart. How could he allow it to occur when he owed her every piece of what remained of his life?

Sassy hadn't died due to natural causes; she died because of his lifestyle when she wanted nothing more than for their two lives to become one. She met her fate early solely because of his choices when she gave him her unwavering support, regardless of what his choice of actions would lead to. So, wasn't he supposed to at least give her all of him? To offer her the assurance that no matter what happened, she'd always be his love? His one and only forever?

Ace was lost in confusion. Her words echoed in his mind. *"Live for the both of us."* But how could he when every day was a fight to keep from putting a bullet in his own head? The guilt was overwhelming, a constant reminder that he had been the architect of their downfall. He had promised a future, only to destroy it with his own actions. The harsh reality was that he alone was to blame. Now, as he teetered on the edge, he wondered if he could truly live for both of them.

"I love you, which you pretty much already know. I'm sorry for everything, Sassy, then and now. I fucked up, and I can't fix it. Hopefully, you can see and understand my heart. Understand my careless decisions. This with Ariel can never replace what we shared, but it can reflect what we wanted." Ace smashed away a tear in the web of his eye. His voice faltered as the weight of his words settled in. "I just need you to know that, even with everything that's happened, you'll always be the one I carry with me. Every choice I make, every step I take… it's all in your memory, for you."

He took a deep breath, struggling to find the right words to say goodbye, even though he knew it was impossible to ever truly let her go. "I'll keep fighting, Sassy, for what we dreamed of. I'll make sure your sacrifice wasn't in vain. And maybe, just maybe, when it's all over, I'll find a way to make peace with what I've done."

Ace stood there for a moment longer, staring down at the gravesite, begging her for the forgiveness of his transgressions. For his thoughts, his actions, his heart. It was more than overdue. He let the silence wrap around him like a blanket, holding onto the last bit of connection he felt with her. Then, with a heavy heart, he turned away, knowing that the path ahead was one he would have to walk alone, carrying her memory like a burden and a blessing all at once.

Sitting in the rental a moment, he stared off in the direction of her gravesite, then an incoming call brought him back to reality. Snatching it up from the passenger seat, his eyes read the caller ID.

"Yo," he answered, seeing it was Whiteboy.

"Say, where you?"

"Bout five minutes out. Why? What's up?"

"You already know a nigga tired of waiting on yo ass."

Ace tried to smile at the remark, knowing he was going to say that. "Nigga, you must got somewhere to be?"

"*And* people to see," Whiteboy chuckled.

"Man, bye!" Ace ended the call. He was grateful for his ride or die and hated the lil situation which took place hours earlier. Both of them had become blinded by their emotions, getting a little bit too caught up in the moment. Was there a set of brothers that didn't fight? However, him and Whiteboy had never. Hell, he couldn't think of a time when they'd actually argued with one another. Their friendship was different from the ordinary. He now couldn't help but to smile, knowing it would be only a matter of time before one had to show the other who was *big* brother.

Putting the vehicle in gear, Ace huffed at the thought of him letting his brother — from another mother — get the ups on him in any type of way. "Boy, stop!" he said, stomping down on the accelerator.

After the twenty-minute drive, Ace caught sight of the rental Whiteboy was driving. He sped the car down the wrong side of the street, sliding to a screeching stop a few meters away from Whiteboy.

He stared at Whiteboy, who smiled, as the smoke from the burned rubber passed between them. Slamming the gear in park, Ace continued to idle the car's motor, wanting to hear it growl. He wished like hell that the car had been an old school with a four hundred block motor.

Whiteboy smiled amusingly, opening his door.

Fully aware of the presence inside the car he drove, Ace motioned his hand for Whiteboy to stop where he was. He'd obviously forgotten.

"What you got going on?" Whiteboy asked as they both got into Whiteboy's rental.

"Shit, just showing you. Go on and get ready for this shit, boy!"

"Nigga, please. Where yo body at?" chuckled Whiteboy, who was about to grab Ace until he slapped his hand away.

Ace had to admit that his one hundred sixty-five pound frame was nothing compared to Whiteboy's physique. But he understood as well that no weight ever matched the superiority of the mind. True enough weight gave you power, yet it was nothing without smarts behind it. And without brains, weight was just weight, a burden to be moved when necessary. His hands balled into a fist, pounding them lightly into the side of his temples. "This all the body I need," Ace said, overly confident.

Whiteboy wanted to laugh. "On everything," he began, glancing up at the roof, "this lil boy done went crazy. Boi, you gone need Allah!"

"Man, please! What the fuck ever. Anyway, nigga, what's the word?" questioned Ace, hoping he'd confirmed what was already in his mind. That would make things less complicated.

"Shit." Whiteboy shook his head like he couldn't even muster up the right way to spew — anything. "Nobody knows shit about it. Everybody saying they saw him show up at the party but nothing else. No hanging with or talking to any females or niggas. It's almost like he showed up, went to the bathroom with no one noticing, which I find hard to believe. But it's like he whacked himself."

"Shawty, that shit sound crazy," Ace returned unbelievingly. Keith's name was ringing a little louder in his head.

"I know. I mean, shhh… It's impossible for somebody not to see or hear nothing at all. The fuck. But I didn't either." Whiteboy began to shake his head again, disappointed. He called himself watching out for unexpected trouble the entire night. He had missed it when it had been under his fucking nose the whole time, happening only some feet away.

Ace could see how he was feeling. How had something of that caliber gone down at the event they threw with so many people around and not one person know anything? Of course, the music was loud, but niggas were drinking, which meant the bathroom would be the most frequented place in the building. Niggas could have been laying. *Ferocious niggas*, Ace was thinking. Yet they weren't that good to catch Dre in the restroom, especially when he had his tool. Nah, whoever had done it had to do either one of two things. One, stumbled across the perfect opportunity and took advantage of it. Or two, had known Dre on a personal level, which was why he didn't see them as a threat, and they used that against him.

"Damn, what the hell was you doing, bro?" Ace asked no one in particular. He became frustrated with the fact that somehow Dre had been caught down bad.

"That's what I'm saying." Whiteboy tapped his finger against the door panel. He was dying to know what had actually happened.

Ace glanced over at him. "So, who you think we take aim at first?"

Whiteboy gave him a look as if to say, *Is that a question?* Then, he said, "Shid, you already know who."

"And what if he not responsible?" Ace couldn't help but to become appreciative. He was glad they were on the same page, and even more so, he was grateful because Whiteboy had paid attention and saw it from his perspective.

"Shid, he just the first," he answered nonchalantly.

"Bet. Tomorrow, I'ma handle this ho…"

Whiteboy cut in. "What you mean *you* gone handle her?" That statement sounded a little foreign to him.

"This shit personal, bro. Real fucking personal," Ace told him, pulling out the pistol and checking the chamber. He'd saved this exact bullet for her — well, unless something popped off between now and then. "I need you to sit this one out. She for self, but I need you there in case there's back up. I already got it mapped out, so just follow my lead, bro. Then, right after, no waiting or shit, we gone serve these niggas. Shawty, niggas got to die."

Whiteboy held in his chuckle but couldn't hold his tongue. "2pac, 2pac. Damn, nigga, you so gangsta."

"Man, shut the fuck up." Ace laughed, pushing his shoulder. "Say, we gone grab the stuff from the spot and load up. Then, we gonna let fate run its course."

"Aight, say less. Tonight though, I'ma grab a hotel room, aight?" Whiteboy said after a second or two.

Ace gazed at him, confused. "What?"

"I'ma grab a hotel room tonight and let you and Ariel do y'all lil romance thang. Y'all need some space to yourselves, you know?" he said, appearing more sincere about it.

"Man, you tripping. Ain't no way you just said no shit like that," Ace returned dismissively as he turned his head away from him.

"Nah, straight up, bro. This ain't no funny shit or nothing, but y'all got y'all own thing going on. And on some real shit, my nigga, earlier when you were standing there, staring at her, I seen that look on your face only one time before." Whiteboy paused briefly, feeling like he didn't have to say that because Ace knew from the start what he was talking about. Then, he continued. "Shawty, listen," he gripped Ace's shoulder and applied a little shake, "you guys need this. You need her, and she needs you. Just be happy, my nigga."

Ace had expected him to say all types of stuff, never this though. Definitely not this. However, it made him want to smile. "And what you need?" he questioned, not knowing what else to say.

Whiteboy smiled broadly before responding. "That muthafucking cannnassshhh!"

CHAPTER 3

"FAX ME THE INFORMATION..." she said into her Bluetooth before eating another piece of her blueberry bagel which had become one of the main reasons for her visits to the Lenox Mall food court. Every time she purchased one, it reminded her of when her mother used to bake them for her and her two brothers to start their days off. Her mother always said, "Something in the stomach makes the brain start pumping." It was corny, but man did she believe it. It seemed like every time she mouthed a bite down, bright ideas would spring to mind, something which made her good at her job.

Whenever tough investigations were slapped in front of her, she'd leave it alone until the right meal filled the depths of her belly and only then would various solutions crowd her cranium. Sophia had the slightest idea as to how she did it because nobody in her family had acquired such a skill. Nevertheless though, she was more than grateful for it.

The Solution, she titled it, often came handy at times like now. After hearing Swift's words, along with making it halfway through her second bagel, she'd already begun to calculate the necessary moves to achieve what had been at the forefront of her mind for every bit of a year and a half now.

They had pulled off their biggest heist ever, but it unexpectedly landed them at the top of a mafia family's hit list. And they would stay there unless they returned the loot — along with the interest they were struggling to keep up with. But it wasn't as simple as saying, "Oops, sorry about that. Here's your stuff back with a little something extra." They had stolen something that was then stolen from them thanks to a sneaky, greedy partner who skipped town with it all, leaving the rest of them to bear the burden and face the consequences.

Though that was only the beginning steps to healing the deep wound they'd caused. The other thing taken couldn't be replaced. And yes, it was a *thing* they'd otherwise be dead for had not the D.E.A. title marked their heads along with the aid of some finger pointing at the absconding villain and the actions of a treasonous son.

However, she clearly understood that it would only be a matter of time before someone within the family asked for nothing less than their heads for the grave transgression they'd made. You could place value on a thing and give a thing of equal value back to make amends, but there was nothing to give that could equate to a life. This was why she was preparing ahead of time, especially after finding out she would be bringing a life into this world. This new chapter in her life brought with it new motivations, giving her a lot more reason for her to execute what she intended to once they located Enzo's treasure as it was called.

She smiled, ready to finish this once and for all. Placing another piece of the bagel into her mouth, she listened as Swift continued to tell her the miscellaneous stuff like the hardship he'd gone through to find their traitor. Sophia could care less about the vicissitudes he suffered on his journey. His journey could have easily been prevented if he'd done what she'd repeatedly insisted before Spencer's fleeing across America with all of *their* fortune. It was Swift's mess, so she was leaving it up to him to gather it back into one big, huge pile.

"Okay," she said, tired of the valueless words. "Swift, let's be clear about one thing. We're going to finish this with no more interferences." Right now, she was trying hard not to remember everything he'd manipulatively insisted would solve their problems — like settling the debt they'd incurred while at the same time setting her up with enough money to plant her seeds amongst the stars and him enough to save what was left of poor little Lily's life.

Suddenly, she remembered the sole reason for them going down this road in the first place. Swift's daughter, Lily, had fallen ill abruptly, and at the time, Swift was desperate. The news of her diagnosis hit him like a wrecking ball, shattering the strong, composed man everyone knew him to be. Swift, the leader of their D.E.A. unit, had always been the one to keep them grounded, the one to make the tough calls, but this was different. And he was different. His world was crumbling and with it, his resolve.

Yet, without hesitation, the team obliged to help him in any way they could. He had made sacrifices for each of them a few times. They had seen Swift's unwavering dedication to them, so they couldn't let him face this alone. One by one, they agreed to go down a path none of them had ever considered before. It started small — bending the rules here and there to gather the money Swift needed for Lily's treatments. But as time went on, the stakes grew higher; the risks became greater.

Before they knew it, they were knee deep in a world of corruption and murder, which they had sworn to fight against. For Swift, it was more than just for Lily — every decision and every compromised principle was also fueled by a darker, more selfish motive. Swift had always possessed a greedy nature, and in the midst of his desperation, he saw an opportunity. Not only could he save his daughter's life, but he could also secure a future free from financial worry. He made it clear to his team that, if they played their cards right, they wouldn't just save Lily — they'd all walk away financially stable with more money than they could ever dream of.

So far, nothing had turned out the way he said it would — and wasn't, she finally concluded. His decisions had only caused more damage, which in turn lead toward more unwanted and unneeded obstacles being placed before them and their whole entire goal. Swift's practical and avarice mindset had caused their team to undergo a tremendous amount of difficulty and mishaps, forcing them to do things to various people — unintentionally — and even to those who were employed by their very own agency. Collateral damage was what he'd called them.

At this point, Sophia had reached her breaking point. She could no longer play the fantasy role in someone else's twisted imagination, acting out scenes that felt ripped from a dramatic cop show. Somehow, fiction had bled into their reality, blurring the lines between what was real and what was absurd. Never in her wildest dreams did she imagine she'd have so much blood on her hands — some of it placed upon them indirectly. They had taken the lives of both the innocent and the guilty while failing to obtain what they were reaching for.

Money, some claimed, was the root to all evil, but others considered it to be the seed bringing forth all happiness. Both she knew were true and as well knew they came with unforeseen price tags. At the beginning, only one objective was on their minds while they cruised this little, turned long, voyage. And as time continued, it seemed as though they had deviated from the set course. Now, after it all, they had accomplished nothing besides the acts of kidnapping, treason, and murder on levels she never would have imagined possible. Sophia, being one who was deeply inspired by Malcom X, understood that sooner or later, the chickens would come home to roost.

"Bye, Swift," she uttered into the Bluetooth nicely, aware that he'd go on and on, babbling about things of no importance. Taking a small womanly sip from her nutrient water, Sophia touched the screen of her phone to check the time. "Mmmh…" She glanced around, now realizing she had overstayed her visit. A lot longer than usual. Immediately faulting Swift, she began gathering her few items on the table. She became angered a little, but not enough to leave behind the remains of her blueberry bagel.

Moving with a purpose, Sophia serpentined her way through the food court, however not in a way that would draw any attention, especially the attention of the wrong people. She accepted the fact that some undesirables were probably trying to tail her. That was mainly why she never stayed in one spot over ten to fifteen minutes. Plus, she never stayed too far away from the eyes of the public. One particular occurrence forced her to become accustomed to this. It involved certain individuals who were capable of the most heinous crimes known to man — things that were incomprehensible, which was more than enough to keep her on her toes and alert at all times of her surroundings.

Although it had been established that they weren't to be harmed, she couldn't let go of the persona these individuals represented. To her, they were the worst kind of criminals, wreaking havoc and tearing down the fabric of American society to satisfy their covetous desires. She had often heard stories of how Italians, cartels, and Russians — foreigners in general — had exploited the American dream, using thievery, robbery, and murder as tools for survival and their economic ambitions. They were ambitions she had helped them achieve due to her own urges and at other times, on the orders of her employer, the government.

This was the same government that criticized African Americans for being radicalized while offering them nothing more than a subpar education, low-income jobs, and ghettos to call home. Then, it would blame them for the drug epidemic, even though the very ones running the country were often the ones distributing dope throughout America. It was ironic how their 'war on drugs' never reached the doorsteps of politicians.

She often reflected on the hypocrisy, the stark contrast between the public facade and the hidden truths. She had witnessed firsthand how the very institutions meant to protect and serve the public were entangled in corruption and deceit. Her role within this complex web often left her feeling complicit, haunted by the part she played in a system designed to oppress rather than uplift.

Every day, the stories of families torn apart by drugs, the lives shattered by violence, weighed heavily on her conscience. The realization that her actions, driven by her own needs and orders from above, had contributed to this cycle of destruction gnawed at her soul. She struggled with the knowledge that the real enemies were not the ones branded as criminals by the media but those in power who manipulated the system for their gain.

The dichotomy between the illusion of safety and the reality of her actions created a constant inner turmoil. She knew too well the stories of young men and women, trapped in a cycle of poverty and crime, used as pawns in a larger game. The thought that she was a mere part in this machinery of oppression made her question her purpose and her humanity.

Sophia had found herself caught up in a relentless struggle between her duties, her wants, and her conscience.

"Excuse me…" she said politely, almost colliding into an elderly woman who hadn't been there before.

Seeing the need to slow her gait a bit, Sophia pretended to straighten out her purse, breaking her fast stride into a casual step. Reaching the escalator, she gazed around at the civilians behind, who did nothing awkward like pretending to stare off in space or anywhere other than what the norm would do, which trackers made a habit of doing. She was very trained at spotting them, so she knew what to look for. And none of those characteristics were on anybody in the vicinity.

She smiled gladly, placing another piece of the bagel into her mouth, strutting about her regular routine. Moving from storefront to storefront diagonally, she used the windows as reflectors to keep watch on everything behind without having to turn around. It wasn't good to let the watchers know they'd been spotted. This would drive them to better disguise themselves and their locations; that was an advantage she wasn't willing to give up.

Sophia stared into the fifth window at a middle-aged woman who offered her a smile, more like an invitation.

Not wanting her to make her way over, Sophia pivoted around and headed for her next destination. Glancing at her surroundings for the umpteenth time, she left the seventh storefront, quickly bending around the closest corner, exiting through a pair of sliding doors. She fought the urge to glance backwards because there was no need to. The doors she'd gone through always made a loud swishing sound whenever closing.

Outside, a wave of heat hit her like a furnace, intensifying the burning sensation on her skin and fueling her urgency to reach the car. "God!" she groaned, adjusting the Prada shades on her face. Her pace quickened as she made her way down the walkway, grateful for the fleeting shade, even though it barely stretched the length of her path. She dreaded the moment it would end, knowing she had only a few more steps before she was fully exposed to the relentless sun.

The sun wasn't exactly her cup of tea. She hated even standing in it for only a couple of seconds, especially when its blazing rays were sending down excessive waves of heat on her perfect skin. Loathed and avoid were the only two words that came to her mind whenever meteorologists reported a forecast of high temperatures.

"Damn!" she scolded, immediately placing one hand up to block some of the gamma rays from hitting her face while keeping the other hand down in her purse. Another 'necessary' act often repeated when entering and leaving public places. Her fingers wrapped around the federal issued Glock 17 as she quickly strolled through the parking lot, eyes scanning the rows of vehicles for any movement.

Good so far. She smirked, seeing her baby off in the short distance. She was dying to feel the breeze from the AC system. Nothing would be more satisfying at this moment.

Her neck craned as she glanced backwards, making sure all had been the same. *Okay, ten feet away.* She swept her eyes from car to car the closer she got, searching for any signs of life. There existed none — well, other than a pigeon on the hood of one. She'd let him live.

Taking one last look around, Sophia released her gun and began fumbling around for her car keys. She'd always made it a thing to keep them on top of everything else because there was no telling when she'd be in a predicament which called for rushing. Yet today, they'd fallen rather deeper than usual, causing her to stick her head up for a brief glance forward, over her shoulder, then returned downward.

Snatching them out, a bit irritated, she disarmed the alarm. As she was about to grab the door handle, the voice of someone unknown said, "Say, baby!"

Sophia's hand swiftly went for the Glock 17 as she quickly pivoted on her heels toward the sound. Instantly, she caught the face of a mixed breed, smiling at her with his head out the driver's side window.

"What's up, Mommy?" he asked her, licking his lips like he was

LL Cool James. The inside of Sophia wanted to curse, yet she couldn't be deterred from her objective. In the middle of turning back around, his next words caused her to stop and grit her teeth.

"Damn, bitch! You can't talk, ho?"

Now, I can shoot his ass, she told herself, forgetting that she couldn't afford the smallest interference. She wasted no time in flashing her firearm, so he could get the picture of disrespecting this particular bitch. Just as fast, she heard something tap against the hood of her car, along with the quick shuffling of sneakers across the asphalt. Before she had a chance to swing the Glock fully around with the rest of her body, she realized how slow her reflex had actually been.

The individual moved swiftly with accurate precision, shoving the barrel of the pistol into her neck, catching her arm with the gun, keeping it away from his direction, while shoving his body up against hers.

The coldness of the steel shot a shiver of fear through her anatomy. *Fuck!* her mind screamed as she stared into the eyes before her.

"Don't," whispered the man. He wore regular clothing with a hat that stopped just above his eyebrows and a scarf which ran from the bottom of his eyes down the rest of the length of his face. There was nothing for her to see besides his skin complexion. "Drop it."

She could only pray to God for help as she released her only defense. She prayed it was just one of those small-time muggers who wanted nothing more than her purse.

But there laid a strange silence between them which made her think it was something more at play than just a simple robbery. Usually, according to news reporters, a thief would rush to get what they were after and be on their way. But quite obviously, this guy wanted something more. His eyes were cold, saying that a purse was the furthest from his mind.

Shaking her arm, he caused her purse to slide off after he took one short step backwards with the muzzle of his gun keeping its place as he kicked the purse then pushed it up under her car. All hopes of her defending herself left when the gun flew away from her hands. It was definitely clear his mental contained something else. She had nothing left in her possession besides one thing, and there was no way in hell she'd give it up voluntarily. She'd die first.

"Get in…" he growled menacingly, nodding toward the driver's side door.

Sophia's mind conjured a few advantages she'd be presented with while making her move to the door. However, her pregnancy limited its success from zero to none if she didn't want to hurt the life inside of her.

Taking her first step, the perpetrator felt the urge to give her a reminder. "Don't fuck around cause I won't hesitate to slump you."

Her mouth uttered only one word. "Okay." She knew he definitely would make good on his words if he thought about performing a sexual act on her.

Opening the BMW's door, he pointed the gun, giving her instructions to unlock the rest of the doors. Pausing momentarily, she waited to see exactly what he had planned because if she got in the driver's seat, it would be impossible for him to commit any kind of perverted act. Gladly, she pressed the unlock button. She glanced over at him as if she'd been waiting on her next orders, wondering where in the hell was mall security when you needed them.

"Get the fuck in…" he snarled, shoving the gun farther into her neck. Her eyes stayed on him a second longer before she sat down, placing her feet on the floorboard.

Quickly, he snatched open the rear door after slamming hers. His weapon ruffled the hair on the back of her head, touching her skull, as he got in. "Hands on the steering wheel," he insisted aggressively, keeping his pistol in position as he scooted to the middle.

She watched him in the rearview mirror while wondering about the other, smaller Glock the agency didn't have knowledge of, which sat a mere few inches away from her in the console. She doubted she'd be able to grab it and fire before he killed her. Time would have to stop for anything even close to that to occur. She was a pregnant woman. Nothing could work in her favor, she knew, staring into the eyes of her abductor. "What do you want?" The question lingered in the atmosphere for a minute or two without a response. It was as if he wanted whatever was on his mind to come as a surprise. Hell, she thought this had been enough of a surprise already.

"Like you don't know," he smartly remarked, slowly dragging down the scarf, exposing his face.

Oh, God, no… Her heart began pounding harder with every minute that passed. Never had she expected to see his face. Not in a million years. Yet here he was, sitting comfortably in her backseat with a pistol against her cranium.

Many questions with no answers came to her mind, while all her hope of surviving flew blindly out of the window. Her death at this point seemed inevitable, she realized. They had taken someone close away from him and had almost sent him with her — should have sent him with her.

Her hands clutched on to the steering wheel tighter. She wanted badly to at least make an attempt for the Glock .26, fully aware of the circumstances now. Her and her unborn's lives could be ended at any given moment. But as well, she knew he could have easily done that already and been out of sight before anybody noticed. Yet he was sitting in her car, being the only one who knew the reason for the prolonging.

"Please…" she began but was quickly cut short.

"Shut the fuck up," he snapped, not caring about her pleas. His ears wanted to hear nothing besides the answers to his intended questions. Another moment of silence passed before he spoke again. "I wanna know everything and every fucking person."

Sophia's attention ran through the windshield as she weighed all chances of surviving this — chances that probably seemed farfetched in the eyes of the passenger. However, she hoped it would be some rather than none, especially after she disclosed secrets capable of changing his mind and life.

———

SOUNDS of Ariel throwing up was the only noise resonating throughout the entire apartment. It had been her second time this morning. The previous one caused her to wake from her sleep, and this one had brought up the breakfast she'd consumed a little under twenty minutes ago. She wanted to cry because it had been her favorite meal — strawberry pancakes drenched in cane syrup with scrambled cheese eggs smothered with onions, bell peppers, and tomatoes.

"Damn, man!" she exclaimed, thinking that the baked chicken from the night before came up with it. Ariel stood, using the underside of her wrist to wipe her mouth, then turned on the cold water to rinse her hands and mouth. The aftertaste of throw up still roamed around her mouth, making her feel the need to regurgitate for a third time.

After using her toothpaste and brush, she had an urge to fix an identical meal, but damn, it would be arduous to repeat it all over again. Back in the kitchen, the aroma continued to linger around, making her second guess the task. She brought herself to a stop, glancing at the cabinets and refrigerator, musing over what to treat her tummy to. Whatever it was would have to be light, yet enough to satisfy her hunger now, and it definitely had to be tasteful.

No more than five minutes later, she'd found the perfect solution to her problem — Fruity Pebbles and a thick layered syrup sandwich. "I need one of those Craig bowls." She laughed to herself, thinking of her all-time favorite movie, *Friday*.

She placed the carton of milk next to the cereal box then the cane syrup next to the Sunbeam bread. "This about to be real good," she told herself, pulling out a big ass bowl. Pouring up a bowl full, Ariel stared down, savoring every bit of it. It smelled so fucking good to her. Drowning it in milk, she took the bowl and her sandwich into the living room and flopped down on the couch, more than ready.

Ariel picked up the remote control. "Wonder who's killing who today." She flicked through channels, pausing at CNN, then after a few seconds, she moved on to Fox. News had been a big thing for her ever since she was young. She loved to see what was taking place around — but outside of — her world. It fascinated her to watch some of the craziest things happening in places she'd never heard of. However, she understood a majority of the stuff they showed were lies though. Nevertheless, it was the best entertainment by far.

"Boring..." she uttered after listening to Democratic and Republican parties exchange words in their fake ass debate about God knows what. Placing another spoonful into her mouth, Ariel read the small words running across the bottom of the screen. That was usually where you'd find the good stuff. "Israeli defense forces bombs U.N. school, killing..." She was reading when two hard knocks crashed against the apartment's door, startling her.

She quickly sat her bowl down, wondering who in the hell was knocking like the fucking police. Grabbing her pride and joy, she didn't remember inviting anyone over. She never had, for that matter, yet some muthafucka with a heavy hand was right on the other side. Ariel only hoped it wasn't the police as she snatched the slide back on her gun. In a few seconds, she would know who exactly this imposter was.

Stepping up to the door, she could see the little speck of light coming through the center, learning a long time ago to never use the peephole nor hold the middle of the door down when unknowns were on the opposite side. She wished Evet would have known it and hated that her friend's unforgettable demise had been the price of such a valuable lesson. Yet she'd been very grateful for it. It had saved her life twice so far.

Two more knocks echoed through the apartment, causing her to aim at an angle in case she did have to let off, so she wouldn't be that far off target.

"Who is it?" she asked, finger pampering the trigger.

"Kero, girl!"

"Kero?" She wondered what the hell he was doing showing up without calling first. But then again, this was Kero's rule breaking ass.

"Man, you act like you'n know my voice or something," he snapped.

"Nigga, I don't." She smirked, tucking the pistol into her waistband and under the big Bulls jersey she had on. She unlocked it but left the small security chain in place, opening it to the length of it.

Instantly, she caught sight of both him and Spain, the magical dumb duo. "Act like you know the magic word." She smiled a little.

"Shawty, open this muthafucking door," he hissed smartly, chuckling after.

"Short, dumb shit. I said *word,* not words."

Kero put his fingers up to his chin. He gazed upward, as if thinking about it, then responded, "Pussy."

"No, sorry… it's not of you today," she said, twisting her lips.

Kero smacked his teeth, releasing a deep breath. "Man..."

"Shut up, crybaby," she told him, slamming the door in his face to undo the chain.

Kero hurriedly brushed past her. "Lil' girl," he remarked over his shoulder.

"I'ma grown ass man, what? You don't see this dick?" she returned, clutching the crotch of her sweatpants, jerking it toward him. Her and Spain shared laughter while Kero waved both of them off.

"You in here smashing, ain't you? Probably why yo ass in a good mood," he told her, on the verge of scooping up her bowl.

"Nigga, don't — unless you wanna feel Becky," she exclaimed, lifting the jersey enough to reveal the pistol.

"Damn, Ariel, you gone kill me bout some punk ass cereal?"

"I've killed dudes for less than that," she said, turning him away from her second meal of today. "Anyway, why are y'all here so early?"

Kero slouched down onto the couch. "Ace told us to pull up."

Ariel gave him a look like, *"Be for real, this early?"* Putting her eyes back on the TV, she said, "And he told you that?"

"So, he didn't yesterday?"

"This early?"

"He didn't say a time, smart ass," he returned smartly, taking out his phone.

"And you don't know his reason either?" she questioned before downing another spoonful of cereal.

Kero released a big huff, tiring of all the interrogation shit. "Ion know, so you tell me?" he spit out, dropping the touchscreen to his lap, leaning toward her.

Ariel noticed the movement in her peripheral, yet she kept her attention focused on the plasma. "It was nothing that had to do with," she paused, grabbing the remote to display the time, "ten a.m. in the fucking morning. I bet that."

"Man, what's up with all the extra shit, A?"

"Shid, you tell me? This for damn sure is a first."

"Oh, what? Like I never come to this bitch," Kero hissed, snatching back up his phone, receiving a text.

"Never this early."

"And that's a problem?"

"Yeah. It's fucking up my me time," she snapped as if she took on an attitude, finally cutting her eyes at him.

"Shhh… It's fucking up my me time too," he said mockingly, trying his best to imitate her voice.

She tried to hold in her little laugh but couldn't due to the way he'd said it. "Shut up…

"And what you think you doing?" she asked Spain, who was in the process of pouring himself up a bowl.

"What? I'm hungry as hell…" he replied without offering the slightest glance backwards.

"And let me guess, yo greedy butt want a bowl too?" She turned her gaze on Kero, who'd been typing something into his touchscreen.

"Who? Shid, I ate," he responded with a slick smirk.

She gave him an evil look. "You dead ass wrong. How you gone eat and not feed him?"

"Nah, that nigga got money. He grown as hell. Fuck you expect me to be? His daddy?"

Before she had a chance to say anything, Spain took off. "Nigga, ain't nobody said shit bout you being nobody daddy. But nigga, you could of stopped like a nigga asked you too. Hell, you wanted to rush over here just to fucking wait. Lame ass nigga."

Kero smacked his lips. "Nigga, you shouldn't of been wit all that sleepy shit."

Ariel sat there, staring at the two, as they continued going back-and-forth. Their words, though, were tuned out, leaving her mind to focus on what had come out of Spain's mouth. *"You wanted to rush over here."* It replayed itself the same exact way he'd said it. She glanced sideways at Kero, who hadn't noticed her awkward side look, wondering what was so urgent to make him be in such a rush, especially if there existed no need to. Her mind rewound backwards to what Ace had told her, along with what she already knew. She could see nothing which would cause for it. The instincts were nagging at her, not letting her brush it off to the side as something random.

Something was up. She just didn't know what. The first rule was to never get caught. The second rule was to always be suspicious of everything new and sometimes of the regular. And most definitely she took heed to the latter more than anything else.

"Man, whatever, lame ass nigga!" She heard Spain say, springing her back from her reverie.

"Fuck nigga!" Kero spit back at him, like he was irritated.

"Both of y'all shut up!" she told them, playing the mama role.

Both in unison eyed her like, *"Who you talking to?"* Realizing she'd have to speak before either of them, she quickly added, "Yep, I'm talking to stupid is and stupid does." Then, she got up to trash the remaining milk in her bowl.

Upon standing, she quickly glanced over at Kero, trying to get a peek of what and who he'd been texting. It was to no avail because of the angle he held his phone in. This became another suspicious headline. Kero messed with a few girls, though never tried to hide that, which he obviously did now.

She shifted her gaze to Spain, who she knew couldn't hold water, especially not when it came down to his facial expressions. And like she expected, it revealed something other than his normal self. *Okay, now what the hell these two got going on?* she asked herself, watching how Spain's eyes were purposely avoiding her, staying locked on the cereal in front of him. It was a natural and unintentional thing for people to look up whenever something moved within three feet. It was a reaction that couldn't be helped unless they were aware and purposefully kept themselves from fixating on it.

That muthafucking cereal ain't that good, she thought, spilling the milk into the sink. Turning the knob on the faucet, Ariel peeked over her shoulder. Kero's phone still held his undivided attention, and Spain continued to snack. Her movement, she made casual, with hopes of catching sneaky eye contact between the two, like niggas did when scheming on one. There wasn't any.

Turning, she smirked, rinsing the bowl, amused at how cool they were playing it. Then, she heard Kero say, "Say, Ariel, Ace and White handling that lil situation, ain't they?"

Ariel paused for a second before responding. *What possessed him to ask that of all things?* She didn't recall Ace mentioning that he told someone besides her and Whiteboy about *it*. Another suspicious thing to add to the list. "You tell me?" she replied dryly, shaking the small droplets of water from the bowl before placing it in the dish drainer.

"Man, why you so-so this morning? I was just asking."

"Yeah, asking something you already know." She wanted to play him, see how he'd respond. *This should be good.*

He looked at her as if he was about to say something dumb, but the only thing that came out was, "Man, aight. You on some other shit."

Ariel glanced at both of them, remaining by the sink, wanting to know what they had on their minds. Another thing she hated was being around secretive muthafuckas. They were capable of anything when plotting on a victim. Meaning, by her being the only one left out of the loop, she was the intended victim —_either directly or by circumstance, which meant indirectly.

She refused to be either; however, maybe she was a little too paranoid. Thinking a little too hard. A little too pessimistic. This was Kero and Spain, who were like little brothers to her. Who she never would ever think were capable of throwing harm her way. Somehow though, skepticism was getting the best of her and refused to subside because of their history. The words of Ace last night were ringing to the tune of her feelings.

Niggas are still niggas at the end of the day, she reminded herself, strutting back over to the couch, staring at Kero, who wasn't moving his fingers this time but kept his gaze on the screen, as if he'd been hypnotized.

"Damn, that lil girl really got ya head fucked up, huh?" Ariel chuckled with a devious grin. She wanted to see his reaction.

"What girl?" he mumbled. If it wasn't a bitch, then who? She was determined to find out and would if she continued to play on his intellect.

"Boy, that girl you been texting since yo ass sat down." She sounded normal, a little less interrogative. She wanted him to feel comfortable to some extent, hoping he'd reveal something.

Sounding a little hesitant, he shook his head a bit. "Oh, nah. It ain't nothing like that."

Ariel reasonably expected his remark. This would do nothing but make her apply a little more pressure. The card she was about to play next had the power to make any nigga overreact senselessly. See, saying the right words, she understood, at the right moment, had a way of causing people to exude so much emotion that it would leave only a small portion of room for them to think logically. This was the most perfect stratagem to use whenever skeletons needed to be let out of the closet without having to lift one finger.

"So, you te..." Aaliyah's *One in a Million* began to play loudly from her phone. She peeked over the arm of the sofa, already aware of the one person who'd been assigned that specific song. Ariel smiled, reaching over. "Yes..." she answered with her sweet voice. Listening closely, she cut eyes quickly at Kero before he noticed then back to the flat screen. "Oh, that's what's up."

Ariel's insides twisted and turned because of the words Ace iterated into her ear. Feeling both sets of eyes on her, she knew to throw them off, especially if this explained the reason for their actions. "Okay, we can do that as soon as you get here. Cool. I'ma go grab the stuff now, bae." She put on a fake smile, giving it to both of them as she stood.

Their stares locked in on her, more than they had the entire time they'd been there. *This is real deep*, she told herself, stepping past Kero, not wanting to make the news breaking news obvious. "Dang, I love you..." she let out as if he was doing the most on the other end. Ariel scratched her head, playing her part perfectly. She stopped a few feet from her car keys, which laid on the kitchen counter. Taking a glance backwards, she noticed Spain had ceased eating. *Yeah, this definitely explains it.*

Moving her gaze to Kero, she could tell a sudden anxiety had entered his demeanor. He now seemed desperate to know what she was hearing. Ariel smiled, thinking she might be able to snatch the keys and leave without any resistance. But if there was any, she'd be forced to shoot the two people she'd grown to love more than her own family. Though she didn't want it to come to that, she wouldn't lose sleep over it either. Everything had taken a drastic turn two weeks ago and even more so in the last minute or two. And their lives weren't nearly as important as hers. So, if it came down to it, death would ensue. No more playing around.

Finally ending the call, Ariel slid the touchscreen into her pocket while moving for the keys.

"What's up?" Kero hurriedly asked, scooting to the edge of the couch.

Nonchalantly, Ariel swiveled halfway, continuing to smile as if she'd heard the best music to her ears. "Nothing. Everything is good."

Her movement refused to stop as he asked very interestingly, "What he say?"

———

RAGE AND FURY surged through his very bones. His jawbone clenched tighter as he pocketed the phone. Ace wanted to see the impossibility in what he'd just heard, yet it added up too perfectly. *Damn,* he cursed himself for being so blinded, so naïve. So caught up on the *loyalty is everything* adage. How could he not have seen it when the signs had been forever present to the point that a blind person could see it from a mile away? Somehow though, he'd missed it. He let the love mislead him, deceiving him into thinking that it was there, like it had been mutual, when all along… nothing existed on the opposite side besides that of treachery. He refused to even ponder about how long it had been running loosely. At this point, it mattered less.

The seed of treason had always laid within Kero. It only needed the right atmosphere and environment to cultivate in. It did, and the bitch the pistol was locked on, along with her conspirators, had been the excellent fertilizer. His grip tightened around the handle while he continued to stare a hole into the side of her head, ready to hand her what she'd brought on herself.

"Ace..." Sophia looked at him in the rearview mirror, her eyes glistening with unshed tears. "I know what happened. I'm sorry. When I found out that she was pregnant, I swear on my life that I tried to stop it. Stop them." She sobbed from the depths of her soul, tears streaming down her face in countless rivulets.

"But you didn't," snarled Ace through his teeth like he was a vicious wolf ready to rip her apart.

"I tried... I tried." She scrambled for words as she wiped the mascara down her face. "They told me nothing would happen to her. They promised me." She dropped her face into her palms, now thinking about the girl she didn't know was pregnant until it was too late. If she'd known her condition beforehand, there would've been nothing she wouldn't have done to prevent her capture and death.

"All they wanted was you. All he wanted was for you to die..." Her head shook. She didn't want to face reality. How could this be taking place right now when her future with her child seemed so promising?

Ace felt compelled to smile at her current state of distress. He guessed, at the moment, she was wishing they'd gotten him as they'd intended. Hell, he had for a lot longer than she probably did.

Sophia lifted her head. "Ace... we all messed up. We all catered to a mistake that can never be undone. I'm sorry for having any part in it. It has been, and will continue to be, the biggest regret in my life."

Ace instantly caught the subliminal message of what she didn't say, but how could he really give a fuck? Like she said, *they* all messed up, and the Reaper was here for her to collect a past due debt. "Stacey, I don't need your apologies — and she don't either."

"But I do..." Sophia said, for the first time craning her neck to look at him face-to-face. "Ace, I'm pregnant, just like she was."

Ace's mouth parted slightly, his expression one of disbelief. Anger surged within him as he realized she thought her revelation might save her — as if it would prevent her from meeting the same fate as Sassy. What did she think, that letting go of someone who was just as deep in the mess as the mastermind would change anything? But then again, how would he appear in her eyes, the eyes of his soul? He could almost hear what she'd say, could nearly see the way the words would flow from her lips.

There was no doubt Sassy would disapprove vehemently, pronouncing words which would make him regret every thought of running down on a female, especially one carrying a life inside of her. In her eyes, he'd probably fit the descriptions of the people who kidnapped and killed her.

But damn, he was nothing like them, or was he? Throughout most of his life, Ace had executed things on dudes, women, and children that were unforgivable — unforgettable, sometimes even regrettable. However, never had he murdered a female who carried life. For some odd reason, those conditions had been off limits. Well, it seemed that way because the opportunity to do such never presented itself. And had it, before Sassy and their unborn child's demise, he might have quite possibly refrained from initiating such.

Missy, for the most part, played a major role in the installment of such a moral. She'd remind him how he came into the world because she refused to get an abortion, which her father strongly insisted she get. Missy believed that if a life started its process into being, then who besides God had the right to discontinue it? In her opinion, any child inside the womb at least deserved their God given right, regardless of the what not. She made sure he understood that if it wasn't for her belief, he'd have been nonexistent.

Maybe that notion alone was what made him respect it. He could have easily been that inexistent embryo.

"Fuck," Ace cursed himself, hating what he was about to do. His conscience struggled to kick in, but Stacey had helped them destroy his world, so it was only right that he returned the favor. He had promised her —and himself. She'd forgive him for something she would never have agreed to in a million years. But how could he live with himself if he didn't follow through? They started it, so he had no choice but to finish it.

Sorry, Ma, he told her in his head. His finger caressed the trigger passionately. It had been a long time coming.

"Ace…" Sophia blubbered, more like a begging plea. "Please just find some way to forgive me. If not for my sake, then at least for my unborn's. I'm begging you to give my baby a chance."

As if on cue, Missy's words began ringing inside of his cranium, making the task at hand a lot more difficult than he intended. But he didn't intend or expect for her to be impregnated either. Finally, his head dropped with his armed hand arm following suit. Something deep inside was trying to hold him back from the heinous act, though some other string left him no other ultimatum. A war was taking place within him, patiently waiting on him to make a ruling decision on which side would win. *Damn, this is the wrong time to be confused,* he thought, attempting to shake off whatever it was.

So many thoughts were crowding his mind, emerging more like little voices of disgust, conviction, and persuasion. *Fuck!* he cursed himself for the third time, finding them complicated to comprehend. It was similar to the stock exchange, a bunch of words pronounced with hopes of being heard over the others.

Ace closed his eyes, wishing he could settle them though grateful for not being able to. The last thing he needed was for something to influence him toward a direction he'd later beat himself up for taking. *No fucking way!* His mind had been made up for over a year now; he wouldn't allow anything to cause deviation. Nothing! They would have to forgive him if there existed a way too.

As his eyelids slowly separated, the mountains of maxims began to fade into the background of nothing. Everything was clear. All had been decreed and destined. All was in.

Ace's cold, murderous gaze locked in on her; his grip tightened even tighter around the weapon. His finger snuggled against the gun's tender spot, ready to help her release that breathtaking orgasm.

"Ac…" she started, but he silenced her before she could fully say his name.

"Stacey… sometimes we do things that are unforgivable. And sometimes we do things that are forgivable. In our way of life, forgiveness is necessary because it makes us human, more capable of dealing with one another after calamity strikes." Ace looked away for a brief moment. "It's almost a basic human need. We live to forgive and pray to be forgiven. A mistake is just that — a mistake —_and mistakes are meant to be forgiven. Nothing — no moral, no murder, nothing — can change that." The pistol quickly lifted, aiming at her skull. Her mouth opened, releasing an inaudible cry. "But likewise, when you're in — you're in — and nothing can ever change that." Nothing else was to be heard or said but that of the pistol launching a bullet into the side of her head. Blood sprayed across both the driver's side window and the windshield as the mechanism exited the front of Stacey's skull. From impact, her body lurched forward, head slumping in the space between the steering wheel and door panel.

Ace looked on, noticing the effect, hating the bullet's course had been through the windshield. That surely made it a *too* noticeable mess.

After staring a few more seconds, Ace swept his eyes around the perimeter, making sure nobody had either seen — nor witnessed — this moment. Whiteboy was a couple of feet away to ensure the same thing. Slowly easing the door open, Ace proceeded in getting out. Taking one more glance at her motionless body, he slammed the door shut. She was the beginning of his revenge, and there was no telling who'd be the end. That would be left up to destiny.

However, he possessed a definite knowledge of who would be next. Someone who wouldn't be hard to find at all. Because this particular individual was at his spot now.

"It's good?" Whiteboy smirked as he got in.

"It's the beginning," Ace returned, pulling the phone from his pocket. Whiteboy gave him an awkward look, maneuvering the truck out of the parking lot. It was quite obvious something serious was on his mental. "Where to?" he questioned, realizing they weren't done.

"The spot…" Ace answered, listening to Kero's ring back.

———

AFTER SWITCHING from the stolen truck to the rental, Whiteboy's driving improved a whole lot. And through it, Ace had run down everything Stacey related to him — every bit of it — from who Paul really was and all about her and her partners' operations, along with the names of the ones who'd snatched up Sassy, one of them being the same one who'd died in Cobb. She mentioned a guy by the name of Greedy Spence who'd vanished with over four point some million and a lot more than that in diamonds after they'd accidentally killed some big mafia figure's son. Then, she told him about the puppeteer named Swift. He'd masterminded the entire thing and been the sole motivation behind Sassy's kidnapping. Most definitely he would be meeting the same fate as Stacey but a little more gruesomely.

Also, she'd filled him in on their dealings with Black and how they manipulated Reno into setting Black up and how he'd killed him. This had been the only thing he could smile about. To him, that nigga was supposed to have been dead and he would had Black not stopped him from doing it.

Lastly came the ultimate blow that had damn near knocked him off his feet. She informed him that Kero had been working for them for almost two years. He was the one who set up the spot to get hit, giving them everything from where he stayed down to his license plate number. He even tried to serve Ace to them on a silver platter by removing the bullets from the pistol right before Ace went to get back Sassy.

Stacey made it seem as if Kero wanted nothing more than for him to be completely out of the picture for good. And her words did exactly what they were intended to do, make his inside twist in pain. It changed the way he perceived life. This was his lil nigga who he grew up with under the influence of Black. A nigga he treated like a little brother and would have died for. Someone he'd killed with just for the sake of eating. And a nigga who was obviously determined to be a true example of the word disloyal.

There existed nothing which could have prepared him for that provoking revelation. One he probably would have ignored had the circumstances been any different. Exactly like he'd done when the signs were evident. Yet hearing it fall from Stacey's mouth made the entire situation more than a mere occurrence. Kero had been fucking him over, serving him the devil's dish of poison, like they'd been long time enemies. And accepting it for what it was, Ace could see no logic in being anything less than reciprocal.

Damn, Fanny. Ace thought of the perfect way to even things out between them in case Kero decided to go missing — which he knew was likely. Kero wasn't dumb enough to stick around. So, Ace would kill his baby sister and her child for the grief Kero had caused. Then, he'd kill Kero himself — very slowly.

Ace stopped calling after twelve calls of getting nothing but the voicemail. "Damn, he might of caught flight." Ace clenched his teeth, running through a list of options Kero had, which was more than he could cover.

"That lil bitch ain't stupid, but then again, he did drop in on Ariel," Whiteboy said, punching through traffic as fast as the situation allowed. The last thing they needed right now was a high-speed chase with twelve.

"Because he knew we weren't there," Ace retorted, the thought looming at the forefront of his mind. He didn't remember telling Kero to pull up. They were supposed to meet later to handle other business, yet for some twisted reason, Ace quickly figured, Kero had done it to cause more damage. He was relieved that Ariel had made it out safely. Lord knows if anything had happened to her, he'd lose it. For real. He would have never forgiven himself for placing her in such a dangerous position because of his own delusional mindset. How could he have thought that trust still existed in this lifestyle? As if there was honor among thieves. That had been his mistake from the start — believing in something that didn't exist in these streets. It was a shame it took all these years and all these losses for him to finally learn not to repeat them. For him to understand that there was no loyalty, only the money.

"Damn it!" He cursed loud enough to startle Whiteboy a little.

"What?" Whiteboy glanced over curiously.

Ace slowly shook his head. "Nothing." He barely moved his lips. The next few minutes of the ride were quiet. Both of them were indulging in their own thoughts. In their own worlds.

Whiteboy knew Ace wanted Kero for himself, and he wouldn't step on his toes when it came to that. But at the same time, he had to draw blood from the lil nigga. In Whiteboy's eyes, Kero hadn't just crossed Ace. He'd crossed all of them. He'd painted red Xs on all their heads, making them the next targets after Ace was torn to shreds. Niggas in this game had one aim — street glory. Everybody wanted to prove they were that nigga, that they were king. And what better way to claim the crown than to commit regicide? This shit resembled the way of life of lions. To become leader of another's herd, you had to kill the dominant male — and sometimes his offspring. Niggas didn't have time for any Simbas running rampant. He glanced over at Ace, who seemed to be any place besides right there in the rental with him. And words didn't have to explain why.

"What?" Ace questioned without even cutting his eyes at him.

"Nothing. Just making sure you straight."

"Hell yeah. But as straight as I'ma fucking be," Ace told him, cocking back the slide to make sure a bullet was in the chamber.

Whiteboy got his point and stomped down on the accelerator, swerving the car into the apartments. He caused a few cars to swerve out of their way. The rental's tires smoked as it came to a screeching halt in front of the building. Not wasting any time, Ace hopped out, sprinting up the stairs, slightly crouched, with Whiteboy immediately following suit. Aiming upward, Ace turned the knob and prepared to cave in the door if need be. But to his surprise, it clicked. He forcefully pushed it open, gun extended, finger anticipating any form of movement.

The hell? He inched deeper into the apartment. Ace wasn't sure if he was walking through the same apartment he'd left this morning. Its current condition definitely hadn't been this earlier. The entire scene looked as if a category five hurricane had swept through, leaving nothing untouched besides the carpet under foot.

Dishes, pots, pans, and all were trashed all over the kitchen. The flat screen had been flipped, along with the couch and coffee table. Ace continued to move into the hallway, realizing that the room would be similar, probably worse. Quickly, he checked the bathroom then proceeded to his sleeping quarters. "This nig…" he began but abruptly stopped because a thought rushed to the forefront of his mind. "Fuck no!" He ran for the closet, hopping over things of no importance at this particular moment.

"What's up?" He heard Whiteboy's heavy footsteps pick up speed.

The closet door was ajar. His heart sank. He didn't have to look to know what he would be missing. Ace could only hope there existed a possible chance that it had been overlooked in the ransacking of the place — regardless of how futile it seemed.

Ace slumped against the threshold, trying to manage the grim smile he displayed. Whiteboy didn't have to ask what they'd taken because his face said it all.

CHAPTER 4

"MAN, shawty, we gone have to kill bra!" Spain exclaimed, shaking his cranium, not believing he had been encouraged to participate in what they'd done. Out of everything he'd done throughout his life, this was by far the stupidest, craziest shit ever. Fucking over Ace had never run across his mind, not even near it, but here he was, influenced by his protégé to pull off something that more than likely would result in their deaths.

So far, they were still breathing at the moment, yet that alone wasn't enough to calm Spain's young mind. He'd run with Ace for some time now, long enough to understand it was always a matter of time before he'd find you then brutally massacre you for all your transgressions. The young boy had witnessed it firsthand on multiple occasions and knew it would be inevitable unless that cup of tea was served to him first. Though he didn't have the slightest clue as to how. Ace wasn't what you would call the average street nigga. He possessed a multitude of traits which stamped dangerously dangerous on his forehead. So, this he would leave up to the one who had insisted on putting them in this predicament.

Kero sucked his teeth nonchalantly. "Nigga, Ion see why the fuck you tripping or stressing that shit. Shit gone be dealt wit real nicely so just chill." Kero was getting tired of Spain's worrying shit. He'd been mouthing the same exact words before they entered the apartment. And now that they were miles away from it, he still repeated the same shit, which Kero couldn't give two fucks about. He could foresee Ace's future and how his demise would come about once and for all. Spain just needed to trust him and fall the fuck back because every time he uttered those words, it made Kero a little more doubtful that Spain wouldn't turncoat on him.

He'd hate to put down his little partna over some paranoid shit. But, if his hand was forced, what had to be done would be done. The last thing he needed was a nigga undoing knots he'd tied so fucking perfectly tight.

"You talking bout chill. After what we just took from Ace? Shawty, be for real. You know, like I do, where this shit finna go," Spain stated hysterically. "I wouldn't be surprised if the nigga already on us."

Kero calmly leaned forward. "Stop bugging…" He grabbed the blunt that he'd intended on postponing until after the lil meeting, but Spain was making that very unlikely by the moment. "And by the way, how the fuck he gone find us?" Kero smirked, glancing backwards at the small safe lying across the backseat.

"Kero, be for real. You know that ain't all his loot."

Kero shook his head disappointedly at all of Spain's hysteria. A bullet probably would be better than this bullshit therapy. "No, nigga, you be for real. You acting like this nigga can just up and make it happen. Like he God or something. Nigga, he ain't fucking *God*. Ain't no different from the rest of us. He bleed too — in case you forgot. He can get a bullet, just like us. Anybody can get it. Ain't no picks and chooses in this shit. What, lil nigga? You don't realize that yet? You see how Black got it? Black was a nigga whose reach went as long as the fucking seashore. A nigga who had real power to make shit happen. And a nigga who got downed. Ace didn't gun him down, remember? He gunned Ace down and still got it…" Kero smiled with a chuckle, hoping the last part didn't have the reverse effect of what he was trying to get across.

"Ace… Ace just survived by a small piece of luck, which was

enough for him to make it through. But it won't be this time. Nah, don't think he Mr. Untouchable or some shit. Because he ain't. He got it, survived, and about to get it again. Period." He paused, wondering how he would take his next words. "Did Dre get it?"

Kero let the question hang in the air, slightly exhausted from the lecture. He stuck the blunt between his lips, about to light it. Lord knows Spain might pass out from a secret he was about to expose.

Spain eyed him closely, a bit angry he'd brought that up. Dre had been a good nigga to him, so he saw no need to throw that in his face as an example. "Man, Dre was different. And ain't no telling how many niggas it took to take him down."

Kero choked on the smoke, trying to contain his laughter. "Niggas?" He needed to gain control of his breath again. "Niggas? There wasn't no niggas. Just one… And nigga, that was me!"

"What's up?" barked Kero, wondering what the hell was his problem and reason for snatching him around so forcefully.

"Nothing much, lil Kero, but I need to holla at you," slurred Dre, presenting an awkward smile while he placed his big arm around Kero's shoulders.

This nigga got to be lit. Kero smelled the liquor strongly as Dre embraced him like he'd poured it all over himself. "Aye, look, I got some other shit going on right now. I'ma have to catch back up with you later, bra," Kero told him as they stepped out into the hallway at Coan Park gym.

Instinctively, his head snapped to the right, peering past Dre's big ass, hoping to catch a glimpse of the duo. But it was to no avail. They'd already vanished.

"Nah, dis shit ain't finna take that long," said Dre, going down the corridor with Kero still under his bear grip.

What the fuck this nigga got going on? Kero thought, releasing a deep breath between his blow out of his nostrils. This entire situation was starting to make him feel as though something odd — and more than some talking — was about to go down.

Stopping in front of the men's restroom, Dre pushed the door open, gesturing Kero to enter first. Kero had taken nothing more than a foot and a half before Dre shoved him forcefully from behind.

"Man, the fu…" huffed Kero, trying to break his fall. Quickly, he planted his foot to prevent himself from hitting the tile floor. Turning, he saw Dre close and then lock the door behind him.

Kero glared with suspicious eyes. "Dre, nigga, what the fuck you got going on?"

At first, Dre refused to respond. He only stood there, staring at him, seeming as if, at any moment, he could get on some Michael Myers shit.

"Dre, nig…"

Without a chance to finish, Dre silenced him with the wave of his hand, taking a few steps toward him. "Lil bra, you sneaky as fuck, ain't you?"

"Sneaky? Man, what the fuck you talking about?" Kero sounded a bit taken aback. He seemed a bit offended by the statement. "Bra, you on some drunk shit right now." He moved as though he was about to leave. With no warning, Dre pushed him again, this time harder than at first, causing him to lose his balance. Kero fell backwards on his ass, sliding a little on the tile floor.

"Nigga!" Kero shouted, nervously scrambling back to his feet. It was very easy for him to see that Dre was intending to have some type of physical altercation. Kero weighed at least two hundred and some pounds, less than he did. How was he supposed to equate to a guy Dre's size on some hands versus hands? Impossible when he clearly knew firsthand what Dre was capable of dishing out — all of which was due to his previous years of training.

Kero gazed at Dre, who hadn't moved an inch, trying to figure out what could he actually do if it came to that. Within that same instance, a thought sprung to mind, something he never thought he'd have to use against Dre. But, if it became very necessary, he wouldn't hesitate a second to use it.

"Bra, what the fuck you got going on?" Kero asked again, trying not to reveal the cowardice which wanted to tread his voice. He definitely didn't want this confrontation.

"Ain't got shit going on," Dre responded with a slick smirk spreading. "The question is what yo ass got going on?"

"The fuck you mean? I ain't got shit going on, nigga."

"Really? So, you don't know what's good wit bra and Keith, huh?"

"Who?" Kero got out, a little dumbfounded.

"Nigga, Ace and Keith." Dre became more heated, knowing this lil nigga was playing, pretending to be clueless.

"Hell nah!" Kero snapped defensively, as if he really hadn't known. Yet he wondered how that could be the motive for all that was taking place now.

"Nigga, please! How the fuck everybody else know, but Kero didn't?"

"Nigga, I don't be knowing every fucking thing the next nigga be doing. What the fuck I look like, the news or some shit?"

Dre closely studied Kero's expression, finding it quite amusing the way he was choosing to play his cards. Kero apparently misunderstood the situation. Loyalty was a thing Dre took to heart, a word he'd dead any dude over who displayed anything close to the opposite of its definition — something Kero was becoming identical with by the minute.

Dre huffed, on the verge of laughter. "Damn, that's real crazy, seeing as how you pose to be the lil brother of him."

"Yeah, the lil brother who he left out. Basically saying fuck 'em. Exactly like he did the rest of y'all."

"Stupid ass boy, you know, like the rest of us, what the fuck bra was going through." Dre cut his own words short, seeing no logical reason to even tread down that road. Why explain something which was self-explanatory? "Never mind dat. It doesn't even matter. Tell me this though. How you come about pushing up to Keith's spot though?"

The question had been unexpected, catching Kero by surprise. How could Dre possibly have known he'd paid Keith a little visit? The business he had going on with Keith had nothing to do with Ace or any of them. Well, at least not until Keith conjured up that nice proposition the other night. It was an opportunity he refused to let pass him by. It would secure the plans he had in mind, giving him more of an advantage than he already possessed.

His schemes had been sidetracked by a swift move Ace made with Black. And Black was too smart for his own good. Too smart to realize his own mistakes in judging muthafuckas. And with that situation playing out the way it had, Kero's efforts seemed to be in vain until Keith became Jesus. Now here stood Dre, threatening it all by the mere sake of knowing — if he actually knew. But didn't he? How else could he have known about the visit to Keith's?

Kero was about to say something to see what he knew exactly. But then, a scene from the last time he'd been out there flashed vividly back into his mind. This nigga was laying, Kero began thinking, remembering the sight of a truck which had appeared similar to Dre's. At the time, he wasn't quite sure if it was Dre's. So, he only brushed it off as paranoia.

Now, at the current moment though, he wished he'd paid more attention and investigated instead of slipping on his surroundings.

Dre patiently waited on his response. He wanted to see what kind of excuse he'd come with. For his sake, he hoped it wouldn't be anything that he might take the wrong way.

"Shawty, really that shit ain't got nothing to do wit Ace or you," said Kero, preparing himself for whatever Dre was bound to throw his way.

"Nigga, stop playing," grumbled Dre, nearly on the verge of popping his head off. "You need to explain."

"Man, we do fucking business together. The fuck you want me to say?"

"Business?" Dre retorted disgustedly.

"Yeah, nigga, who you think I been copping from? Niggas ain't giving the type of deals holme fucking with me on."

"Man, be for real. Who you expect to go for that shit?"

"Nigga, Ion care who go for it. It is what it is. Dude fucking wit me righteously, and I'ma keep fucking wit 'em the same way," Kero spit out but tried to avoid going too far with his choice of words. This was two hundred and sixty some pound Dre he was talking to.

Dre stared at him, gritting his teeth together as he slowly shook his head, wanting badly to fuck Kero's ass up for thinking shit was sweet.

He'd be out of line in the eyes of Ace if he knocked Kero's head off without any form of say from his lips. But damn, he deserved it right now. Smiling once again, Dre said, "Aight, say no mo. I'ma let bra handle it how he see fit." Dre gave him another look then turned toward the bathroom door, about to leave.

Fuck! Kero thought, getting the jest of Dre's choice of words. He could clearly see the type of shit Dre was hinting at and knew better than any of them that if word made it to Ace, he wouldn't hesitate in ordering him to set him up. That, by itself, would definitely dead his vision of the future, which he had mapped out so perfectly. And if he refused, he might as well put the bullet in his own head. They'd insist on nothing less.

Presently, Dre appeared to be a real big threat and an obstacle he'd have to overcome no later than now. Swiftly, Kero snatched out the short combat knife from his pocket. He always kept it on him in times when his pistol was out of reach — like now. Quickly, he moved on Dre, who was reaching for the lock, very unaware of the situation at hand.

Once close enough, Kero leaped onto Dre's back, quickly wrapping one arm around his head while using the other to launch the blade through the side of his neck. A growl erupted from Dre as he backpedaled with his frantic hands clawing for Kero's raging hand that repeatedly thrust the knife into his flesh.

Dre spun hysterically, ramming Kero against the bathroom's wall with every pound his body carried.

"Mmm..." Kero groaned from his head hitting the brick as Dre collided with it a second time.

Catching hold of the arm on his head, Dre yanked it down and twisted it over while shooting Kero a sharp elbow to the ribs.

"Fuck!" he screamed, his mind beginning to panic. Dre was getting the upper hand. Blood cascaded from Dre like a water fountain. Fully bringing the clutched arm down, he pivoted toward Kero, finally catching the bladed hand. Without procrastinating a second, he slammed his head into Kero's face.

Crimson splashed from Kero's nose as his head tilted backward.

Not wasting any time, Dre struck him in the jaw with his elbow then slammed him hard into the nearest wall. He then hit him again with the same elbow, in the same spot. Kero became a little dazed and faded as he began to lift the knife again, but it would be to no avail. Dre quickly seized his forearm, banging it into the brick as forcefully as he could.

"Fu..." huffed Kero in pain, not knowing if his hand that was being beat into the concrete hurt worse than the devastating blows to his jawbone, which he knew would shatter if he issued another one.

Menacingly, Dre stared at him with his bear claw around his throat, squeezing as he slammed Kero's hand once more. The last impact caused the weapon to fly from his grasp.

A muffled sound escaped Kero's lips, like all hope did from his mind. The only object he possessed, the only thing that was capable of guaranteeing his victory, had fallen out of reach. Defeat was quickly becoming the situation. Kero's throat felt as if it had turned into a wet towel which Dre intended on wringing all the water out of. The pressure he was applying had Kero gagging.

Blood continued to cascade from Dre's neck sporadically, forming rivers of chaos. Dre knew his life was exiting with every drop which spewed from him. He could feel it. This nigga gon' die before I do, he told himself, realizing that his strength was escaping along with the tide of life. Determination had his mind set on seeing Kero's execution through, yet reality gave him every reason to doubt the possibility of it. Here he stood, losing enough blood to fill a fucking fish tank, and Kero, as far as he could tell, had at least another minute and some left before he would exit. He desperately wanted to hold on. Dre wanted badly to kill him; however, neither strength nor time were on his side.

Kero gasped, unable to take in even the smallest atom of oxygen. He scratched then sank his fingernails into the skin of Dre's bear claws. Kero attempted to pry his hands off of him. It was to no avail.

The rage within Dre's eyes made all he intended evident. Kero, if he could help it, possessed no intention of letting this nigga kill him, especially after the damage he'd inflicted. His mind was beginning to become dismayed as his lungs screamed for air. Damn, how bad he needed to free himself from death's grip.

Dre's hands were locked onto him like a Pitbull's jaw. Letting his fury become the fuel to his strength, Dre squeezed tighter with everything left inside of him.

Kero sensed his body about to give way to the choking. Becoming weaker and weaker with each second that passed, he knew he had to do something. Anything and fast! Then, a brilliant thought came to mind. Stretching his arm, Kero stuck two fingers out and began to dig into the open wounds on Dre's neck. Instantly, Dre twitched, shaking his head from side to side to alleviate the awkward pain.

A groan escaped Dre's lips as he snatched Kero from the wall, slinging him forcefully into the nearest stall door. Using his weight against Kero's body, the two of them busted into the stall, unable to break the fall which quickly consumed both. Thanks to his size and him landing on the bottom, Kero's elbow collided with the toilet as he fell between the stall's wall and toilet.

"Nigga..." Dre grumbled, unable to fully get his words out due to the condition of his throat. The maneuver had been a bad move on his part. With Kero being as small as he was, he was able to fit perfectly into the small space. And because of Dre's build, he was prevented from keeping his grasp. The toilet and stall wall had seen to that. His adrenaline had been too high for him to think logically before putting himself in this predicament. The move, he now realized, had killed all chances of him paying Kero back for the sneak attack. Staring coldly, Dre gazed down at Kero, who was frantically gulping on all the oxygen he could take in.

Catching some of his breath, Kero wasted no time in striving to slide half his body underneath the stall's wall.

With one hand against the wall and the other clutching onto the toilet, Dre helplessly watched as Kero made a slithering escape. Damn, he had an urge to go fetch the knife. Yet he knew from the weak sensation overcoming his body that it would be futile. He probably would make it to the blade and nothing more than that.

Fuck! It was over with. There existed nothing else he could do besides accepting his inevitable fate. Blood continued to pour from him as his body began to shiver while the icy cool breeze treaded over his skin before penetrating his flesh. Death was at his doorstep and ready to collect. With his eyes locked on Kero, he mustered his last energy left and stepped on Kero's ankle, causing him to stop with a little jerk. He leaned over him, offering him a menacing glare that told him he'd be waiting for him in hell.

Peering up, Kero understood it. He was over. Dre fell forward some, his hand slipping from under his weight. Unable to do a thing, his torso collided into the toilet, finally slumping into its final position. Kero stared a moment, his body still as ever. He wondered had Dre exited the building. His eyes were still open, but nothing moved besides that of the flow of his blood.

This nigga might be playing, Kero said to himself. He wouldn't feel relief until he was for certain. Recoiling his leg slightly, Kero kicked Dre's shin as hard as he could. Nothing besides the targeted leg moved from the impact. With a new grin spreading across his face, he pulled himself fully into the next stall. He was grateful, glad, that death had spared him for the umpteenth time.

Getting to his feet, Kero wasted no time in pushing open the stall's door to leave his once living protégé in the next one. His smile quickly dulled out. Surviving Dre had been a hell of a task, but with every passing second, it seemed to become so minor to the one that was now at hand. The scenery before his very eyes could have easily belonged to one of those serial killer movies. Blood was everywhere in large splatters from the floor to the wall then surprisingly, to the ceiling. Damn, it was a mess and way too much for him to clean up. That would take hell of a time to do and something which he didn't have.

Knowing time was of the essence, Kero quickly moved to the sink to rinse Dre's life from his hands. As the cold water drove the crimson down into the drain, he looked up at his reflection.

"Fuck..." he spit sotto voce, taking in the image. Blood was sprayed all over the front of his clothes, streaks running the length of his neck and arms, specks scattered about his face.

"Fuck..." he let out a second time, stomping his foot lightly, wondering how in the hell he was going to make it out of the gymnasium without being noticed. Impossible! Damn near all the mutha-

fuckas at the party were intoxicated. But it wouldn't prevent them from noticing the distinctive coloring of his clothing. Everybody with twenty-twenty vision would see.

Instantly, he pulled his shirt over his head, hoping that the deep stain missed the white beater underneath. Yet he knew more than likely that it had touched it just as it had the shirt. And disappointment prevailed. The soiled stain appeared to stand out even more so on the white tank top than it did the t-shirt.

He figured it was best to either put the shirt back on or discard the tank top also. "See this shit, nigga," Kero snapped, gazing backwards at the lifeless body. It had been the only good which came out of this.

Great, Dre had been silenced. Bad, he was stuck in the bathroom in need of an escape route. A very secretive one. Immediately, his eyes jolted upwards. He wondered if the boards in the ceiling would be enough to hold up under his weight. And if so, he'd still have the problem of making it past the partiers whenever he came down.

Damn. He turned a bit, continuing to sweep his eyes over the area. Then, as if his prayers had been answered, something he hadn't seen before sparked in his peripheral. "Fucking right!" he exclaimed excitedly, relieved a little bit. He paced over to the two small windows, which were situated at the top of the back wall. Standing directly under it, Kero could clearly see that his height wasn't enough to do what was needed. But regardless of that, he was determined to get it done.

Hopping, Kero leaped and reached for it, but there wasn't any type of ledge for him to pull himself up on. "Shit..." he cursed, sweeping his eyes around the restroom in search of anything that would help. A small trash can, which sat opposite of him in the corner, gained his attention. It seemed to be perfect for what he was trying to accomplish.

Moving the canister directly below the window, he jumped on it, quickly unlatching the latches on the seal. At first, the window wouldn't budge, diminishing his hope a little. But suddenly, it finally gave way. The smell of fresh air rushed into his face, causing him to deeply inhale the aroma of freedom. Kero tugged upwards, on the verge of setting himself free, until something he'd forgotten sprung into his mind. A thing of the most importance.

Evidence...

Spain's eyes grew into headlights. Shock emanated from every piece of his face. There was no way Kero told him that he was the sole cause of Dre's death. For some reason, it instantly became hard for him to avert his gaze. To move his body. To speak with his mouth. To use his brain.

Smirking, taking another pull from the blunt, Kero stared at him a moment. He for damn sure didn't need this. "Listen," he started off, releasing the acrid smoke from his lungs. "Shawty, we in something that has no love for anybody, point blank period. There's only one way to the top, and that's by being heartless. *We* — me and Ace — had to learn that by firsthand experience. By seeing the same niggas who ate at the table get bodied by the same niggas that ate at the same table. This was how *we* were taught. Me and bra know how this shit really go. We the same, but there's one difference between us, Ace is stuck in fantasy land, believing that loyalty lasts forever, when it's only some'n momentary. Me, I'm stuck in reality, dealing with the real, the here and now. Only thinking bout the future whenever it seems to be worth a thought."

Kero took another, longer drag, keeping his eyes locked on Spain. "This game is shell, shawty. And if you intend on winning, you betta learn the rules and how not to get emotionally involved in it. Like Black once told me, *it's bad for business.*" He chuckled, remembering the adage. "And likewise, it can be bad for your health."

With those last words, he extended the blunt to Spain, who hesitated a moment before taking it. Kero could only imagine what was going on inside his head right now. If the shoe was on the other foot, he'd be figuring out a way to subtract another mouth from the table before he was. However, Spain showed no signs of thinking about such. He only inhaled the kush smoke casually, like always, appearing as if Kero hadn't uttered a word. Maybe he was scared or didn't fully grasp the meaning behind his words.

Kero began to think, carefully watching him as he passed the blunt back. Putting it to his lips, he took a strong drag and asked, "You good, shawty?" He needed to see where his head was at.

Staring beyond the windshield, Spain nodded his head slightly, a smirk presented on his face. "Hell yeah. Shit just crazy."

"Boy, who you telling?" Kero returned, giving him another overview. Satisfied, he let the smoke swirl to the roof, wondering if he'd scared him to death — to the point that he wouldn't even think of trying no shit on him. Hopefully, the words hadn't leaped over his skull. Though he knew, murder and the element of shock had a way of causing the reaction Spain was displaying, especially seeing that he was young. It would be a matter of time before Kero realized how wrong his estimation of his young friend had been.

CHAPTER 5

ACE LAID THERE, staring at the hotel's ceiling for what seemed like hours. He thought about yesterday's events and occurrences from years ago. Never would he have thought that he'd be a witness to everything he had after taking those first steps outside of Missy's door. He knew without the shadow of a doubt that had he seen it all beforehand, his actions definitely would have been opposite.

Many times, she'd forewarned him about 'the game'— this way of life — yet he'd wanted the money and power. Both had placed a veil over his eyes at a young age, leading him to wholeheartedly believe that the glamour and fame were his religion. It made it seem as if that was all there was, nothing more. It made it seem like there were no hardships for those on this side of the fence, convincing his immature mind that the winners were on this side while those fated to be losers were on the other. It taught him to never become friendly with the life on the other side unless he was content with poverty like those on that side.

He swore that on the other side was where his true enemies lurked, lying in wait for the perfect opportunity to pull him down, like crabs in a bucket. They would trample him underfoot, exploiting every moment of weakness, until nothing was left of the person he'd fought so hard to become. To him, that was equivalent to dying a coward's death a thousand times — each time more humiliating than the last. The thought of it gnawed at his mind, driving him to push harder, to never let his guard down, because in this game, even a moment of hesitation could be fatal. In his world, there was no room for doubt, no space for mercy — only the relentless struggle to stay on top, no matter the cost.

So, likewise, the traitors, the treasonous, the disloyal — all were the enemy, lurking on the other side. They were to be dealt with by an iron hand and never to be trusted. He put his faith in the words of Jesus. "Those who are not with me are against me." Anyone who wasn't aiding his campaign to the top was trying to bring it down. This belief had been so deeply implanted that it became his very nature.

However, this alone had ended up his biggest flaw. For years, the game had blinded him into believing that those who were on the same side as him were with him. That loyalty existed there. One for all and all for one. Yet that wasn't the case and was only one side of the game, a side he was forced to recognize through detrimental experiences.

From a first-person view, Ace witnessed how it turned out with Kay, who became a traitor, with Reno, who committed treason, then with Black, who vividly proved that there was no loyalty — only the money. And he'd seen the type of shit money was capable of introducing at a moment's notice, the same type of shit the game would allow to balance itself out.

It had been all shown to him, and he'd vehemently refused to acknowledge it. The game had become a father to him, slowly teaching him when he chose to listen and quick to chastise him for his consequential actions. It had done its job in exhibiting the gains, along with the costs of such were to be attained. But him being him, he made the choice to overlook the compensation due, which was always to be paid, regardless of if a nigga wanted to or not.

He was smart. He was Ace, so at times, he thought he understood it all like the back of his hand. Like he'd seen all there was to see in this way of life. Yet it nonetheless proved that he'd only encountered bits and pieces of this shit. No man living had perceived its entirety. And he would soon be forced to come to grips with that. He'd come to realize that it was just something too big to conquer, a thing too fast to slow down, and the thing a nigga could never stop playing once they started.

Ace twisted over onto his side, facing Ariel, letting the words he'd verbalized to Stacey replay in the back of his head. *"When you're in, you're in, and no one can ever change that."* He understood what his fate was to be and as well knew he would have to make the necessary adjustments if he intended on having a future with Ariel and his best friend. First and foremost, he needed to clear a way into that future, starting with Kero and the nigga, Keith. Plus, he needed those diamonds.

Caught up in his thoughts, he didn't notice that Ariel had awakened, staring at him. "I hope you thinking about me." She smiled, sounding like a heavenly angel.

He slid the back side of his hand down the side of her face. "Something like that…" Ace smiled, more than ready to kiss her. He groaned, knowing she hadn't brushed her teeth. "I hope you dreamed about me."

"It was something like that," she returned playfully, happy his face was the first thing she'd awakened to.

Ace stared at her a moment, inaudible. Words had sprung to mind to tell her. But the more he pondered about them, the flashbacks of uttering them to Sassy that last morning found their way into his membrane. It seemed as if the exact same scene was replaying itself out. He was now trying to conjure every option, other ways, around his present dilemma. There existed none. How was he supposed to keep her safe and out of harm's way if harmful ills were directed at him?

He was more than aware she knew how to handle herself in any given situation. She'd proved it countless times. However, the things he faced now were very different from how they were then. And he just didn't have the slightest idea as to how he would really prevail. Ace refused to let her get caught up in the web of his consequences. He uttered a prayer in his head, hoping he'd be able to make good on the words that were about to leave his mouth.

"Ariel…" he began but instantly paused, giving his thoughts another chance to gather. "Look, you already know the life we live and how this shit go… In this game, we live to play and play to live, with no outs. No breaks. None of that shit… It's a luxury to even fantasize about exiting this shit. We," he had to correct himself, "well, I'm in this shit till death do us part. It's my destiny. But you… you…" Before he could finish, she felt the need to correct him.

"I'm in this with you till death do us apart." She gripped his hand gently, lifting it to her lips for a kiss.

Ace gazed at her admiringly. He expected that from her, and it hurt. Though he was grateful. She was a rider by nature, which any street nigga would kill to keep by his side. But right now, he didn't need her to be that. He needed her to be cautious, and his heart wouldn't allow anything less.

"Ariel, I love you, man, and the last thing a nigga want to see is for something to happen to you…"

"Ac…" she began, but he put a finger to her lips this time.

"Listen, I know how you feel, man. I know probably more than anybody that you know how to take care of yourself when it's time to get busy. But I… I love you too much to risk losing you. Ariel, I lost the love of my life one time already, and now, I've been given another chance to experience it. To see a side of life that some never get to see or fully embrace and…" he smiled, refusing to let his eyes shift from hers. "I want too. I wanna be able to say I married the love of my life. To be able to raise a child with that same love…"

He could tell as he spoke that his words were arousing emotions deep within her. Her teary eyes and facial expression said it all. Yet he wasn't finished. "I really want that, but at the same time, I understand that I'd never be able to walk away from this life. This game and the life I want are two worlds are opposites, very different and separate, and when they collide, each possesses the strength to destroy the other." Ace became silent, giving his words enough space to settle inside of her heart and mind. The last thing he wanted was to confuse her or for her to misunderstand.

"Ariel, my life can't change. I'm stuck waist deep in this shit. So, I can only adjust to new events and circumstances. But you, being a female, have a chance at living a new life, a different one. Being someone other than the person you are. A someone without the game.

And just being honest, what female wouldn't want that house with the picket fence, with a husband that supports her, and kids that adore her? Yeah, I know you different — hell, very different." He chuckled, causing her to let a small one out as well while she continued to hold back her tears.

"But Ariel, real shit, I feel as though I'm being selfish by not wanting to change my lifestyle for the one I claim to love. Especially for not having the courage to push away the one I love so that her safety is more than guaranteed. And that's the problem cause I could of never pushed Sassy away and neither can I push you away... I sit here now, fighting with myself about what to do. About what I want and then about what's right. And honestly, I can't truthfully or wholeheartedly decide on either. So, Ariel, right now, you have to make that choice. Please don't be quick to answer. Do me a favor and think about it more deeply than you've ever thought about anything. Do this for me and know that no matter what your decision is, I'll always be here for you however you need me. Think about it, baby girl. Life ain't getting no easier."

Ace bore deeper into her eyes, wishing he could see her soul. His hand passionately caressed her face. At the moment, he hated himself. He had denied Sassy this right — a right she should have been entitled to. She had been his first. Maybe things would have turned out differently if he had. Then again, maybe not. But just allowing her that chance would have been more than worth it.

Kissing her on the forehead, Ace was on the verge of getting out of the bed until she caught his arm, stopping him.

"Ace..."

"Don't..." he quickly returned.

Ariel smacked her teeth. "Boy, I wasn't finna say anything about that. But it's something I want you to think deeply about too."

He looked at her, unsure if she intended to tease or say something on a serious note. Yet her expression said enough for him to want to hear it. Ace looked on attentively.

"Ace, I-I'm..." She didn't have a chance to finish. Ace's phone blared to life loudly, causing both to jump in unison. *This nigga.* He smiled, thinking of the only person he'd assigned that particular ring-tone to. The only someone who always seemed to find the perfect way to interrupt them.

"Yo, what up?" he answered. He listened to the fast chatter through the receiver. His expression dulled quickly into a state of bewilderment. "Hold on..." he said, sweeping his retinas searchingly over the room.

"What's up, bae?" Ariel questioned, becoming concerned due to his suddenly erratic movements.

"Aye, where the remote?" he rambled about cluelessly.

"Here..." Ariel tossed it to him after realizing it was on the floor.

Turning on the TV, he asked, "What channel?" Flicking past a few miscellaneous programs, he finally came to the one he was looking for. His mouth went agape as his eyes locked in on the familiar scenery the news reporter was giving details about.

"Standing here at the corner of Hutchinson Street and Chipley Street, located in a Southwest Atlanta neighborhood, where directly across from me is the house where firefighters responded to a house fire call two days ago whereupon they discovered two bodies that investigators had declared a domestic homicide and suicide..." The reporter's face became a little more focused as she let the brief anticipation settle before her next words. "Yet as of now, they are treating it as a double homicide."

Ace's mouth dropped a little more as he watched pictures of D-nice and the girl he remembered as Keisha spring to the screen. "The bodies of twenty-five-year-old Corey West and twenty-three-year-old Keisha Mills were found late Saturday night after firefighters were called to the property of 3313 Hutchinson Street, which is the house you see behind me..."

"So, why are police calling it a double homicide now, Whitney?" the in-house news reporter asked.

Ace was shocked by what he was hearing. "Well, Hank, the police are giving very little information as to what they think actually took place here Saturday night. But they are mentioning that the male, Corey West, was found there in the driveway..." She directed the camera toward the spot she was referring to. "The female, Keisha Mills, was later discovered within the home. But still not a word as to the cause of their deaths. Here is what Detective Louis Gram, who is the leading detective of the investigation, had to say…"

Ace continued to look on as a previous recording of the middle-aged looking detective came to the screen. "Is there anything you can tell us as to what actually occurred here?" a reporter asked.

"Well…" he began, eyes partially shying away from the camera. It was obvious that this wasn't his cup of tea. "Nothing as of right now, besides that it is being treated as a high profile, double homicide."

"Are there any leads on a possible suspect or suspects since it's being treated as a double homicide and not as a homicide-suicide?"

"No, not at this very moment but individuals of interest are being questioned."

"Can you give us a hint as to why it's now being labeled a double homicide instead of a homicide-suicide as it was at first claimed?"

You could tell by the detective's facial expression that she'd put him between a rock and a hard place. "I'm not at liberty to say. But it is being thoroughly investigated by some of the best officers in the field."

Right when the reporter, Whitney, was about to say something else, the *Breaking News* bulletin flashed onto the screen. The visual switched to the news station studios.

"Breaking news…. Two men are wanted for questioning involving the murder of twenty-eight-year-old D.E.A. agent, Sophia Williams, who was found hours ago shot to death inside of a vehicle parked on the top parking deck of Lenox Square Mall."

The touchscreen fell from Ace's grasp, following suit was the remote control. He couldn't believe that pictures of him and Whiteboy had come up on the television screen. Everything in the world had come to a halt, all except the newscaster's voice. "The men are twenty-three-year-old Anthony Jackson and twenty-four-year-old Michael Turner. If you see them, these men are not to be approached. Contact your loca…"

The rest of the words fell on deaf ears. Ace had heard all he needed to. *Fuck*, he thought. The last thing he needed was for this to happen.

Snatching his phone back up, along with the remote, Ace hit the power button, cutting off the TV. He didn't want to be reminded of the deep shit he was waist deep in now.

"Bra... Ace..." He could hear Whiteboy saying as he placed the phone back up against his ear.

"Man, fuck," was all he could say in return.

Whiteboy's next words were rapid, tumbling one over another. They were too fast for Ace to comprehend when his own mind raced just as fast. "Man, listen. Just stay put till nightfall..." he told Whiteboy before disconnecting the call.

Glancing over his shoulder, he saw Ariel with her hands covering her mouth. You could see the light tremble sliding through her body. She looked as if she was on the verge of breaking down. And he was clueless as to what to say. Shid, he felt the same way as her — lost, shocked, and very uncertain of the future.

Ace sat down at the edge of the bed, rubbing his face. Things had just pivoted from bad to worst in mere seconds. "Damn," he growled, thinking how he would beat these odds — odds that were almost impossible to conquer. Keith and his army, along with Kero, he could deal with. Even the remaining agents responsible for Sassy's death. But the entire fucking domestic army of police was a different thing. There existed nothing on his side of the fence to attempt or even muse over taking on such a force. Then, to top it off, there were patriotic citizens who'd aid in the campaign of their capture — defeat. Nothing about it could be used to his advantage, which meant, without a doubt, it was a lose-lose.

Ace fell backwards, his hands covering his face. He wished he could take it off right now. There — nine times out of ten — was a picture of it being printed and posted everywhere besides space.

"Man, damn!" he hissed through his hands. He now realized he'd fucked up to the hundredth degree. Ariel crawled over to him, lying her head down on his chest, snuggling close against his body like a toddler would do.

"Ace, my mind has been made up since the first day we spoke to each other. I've always accepted every thang that came with you and will continue to, no matter what happens. It is us against all."

Her words touched him yet at the same time hurt him more. This situation wasn't what he wanted for them, especially not for her. However, due to his own selfish ambitions, here he was, placing her in harm's way, exactly like he'd done with Sassy. Though he couldn't push her away, definitely not at a time like this. Regardless of if it was the right thing to do, he couldn't afford it. Definitely not right now. He wanted to see another day, which would depend on her. He would need her — hell, *they* would.

Finally gaining a grasp on his mental, Ace slowly stroked her hair. "We gotta run. Fuck Kero and all that other shit. We gotta leave tonight." Running, he knew, was inevitable in the face of something as big as his current predicament. Likewise, he clearly understood that running took money. They'd need a nice amount, and something to the effect of four million and valuable diamonds fit the picture perfectly. Ace had already run the thought of locating Stacey's ex-partner, *Greedy Spence*, through his mind a thousand times and now saw him as a primary.

Ace reached, grabbing his phone. His mind began to formulate different strategies of how to possibly, yet swiftly, accomplish it all. They would need help to get it done and financial backing for travel. There was only one person he had in mind who could provide both.

"He should be more than willing to," he mumbled a little above a whisper, causing Ariel to look up at him. Ace smiled, seeing the Stacey situation had been both a curse and a gift, delivered to him personally by the devil himself.

CHAPTER 6

Detective Louis Gram sat behind a desk at the zone six precinct, gazing over his latest case information. It had been a little over three hours since he'd moved from the desk loaned to him courtesy of the chief.

Papers and photos were spread about, making it appear as if they were disorganized pieces to a puzzle, which he was having a hell of a time with. Though this particular method was his way of putting investigations together. He had to see everything at one time instead of running over something then having to go back and cross-reference material not in arm's reach. This art which he'd mastered had made him one of the best detectives added to Atlanta's homicide unit.

Gram would sit for hours on end, absorbing every single detail of a crime before even considering forming an opinion or offering a notion of what actually took place. You could compare him — to some extent — to a physician paying close attention to every symptom before delivering a diagnosis. These days, his accuracy in case diagnosis lay somewhere between ninety and a hundred percent.

However, that was only part of the reason why the label "best" was associated with his name. Louis Gram wasn't exactly what you'd call a bureaucrat or a by-the-book guy. He was known for doing whatever was necessary to solve a case, a method that proved to be the perfect remedy throughout his career. He quickly learned how to get things done, how to handle what needed handling, and afterward, how to clean it up without leaving a trace — leaving nothing for the noble men to cry about. Some though, in their official capacities, considered it 'Wild Wild West' mayhem and recklessness by a disastrous rogue. Yet behind closed curtains, those very same ones would nonetheless applaud his handiwork wholeheartedly — sometimes out of sincerity and most of the time out of fear.

Louis though wasn't the type to acknowledge audiences. It didn't matter whether it was congratulations or criticisms, he only wanted them to stay clear of his way. Each case was personal to him, and anything getting in the way of its solving would be dealt with in a personal manner.

Gram studied the photo of Keisha Mills. She had multiple stab wounds on her face trailing down to her torso, passing her navel to the pelvic area. Second-degree burns covered her body, some areas appearing as if the fire had boiled her flesh. He had gazed over the picture a dozen or more times, wondering how such a beautiful girl got caught up in this mess. He laid the photo next to the one of the male who was sprawled out in her driveway, overdosed.

The first detectives assigned to the case had — un-expertly — made a quick assumption that the crazed drug addict had gotten lit, found his way into the home, though there was no evidence of forced entry to support that, sexually assaulted the female, and then stabbed her to death. They surmised that he set the place ablaze before collapsing to his death. It was a tidy narrative, convenient for closing the case quickly, but it ignored the inconsistencies — the lack of defensive wounds on the victim, the precise pattern of the stab wounds, and the odd placement of the burns. Something about the scene didn't sit right with Gram; it felt staged.

Gram shook his head, hating how most practitioners in his field approached cases with a quick open-and-close mindset, leaving the real transgressors on the loose. Had he been anywhere else besides Atlanta working on another, more complicated investigation, this particular case would have been added to the pile. He had been leading an 'off the record' investigation for almost two years now, but this crime, along with the one from the day before, demanded his undivided attention.

The two were linked to some certain person that was — somehow — tied to a particular set of people in his initial case. Honestly, Gram couldn't understand the connection or the reason behind the murders, though he knew he needed to figure it out fast. The body count was only growing and moving in unknown directions. Yesterday's finding of Agent Williams' body verified that much. Gram only hoped his assigned partner, Detective Towns, discovered something which possessed the potential of giving them the breakthrough that would at least make sense of it all. That would be a starting point at retrieving the spilled marbles.

Glancing back-and-forth between the photos, Gram could think of nothing capable of linking the two people besides that of a third party. The murderer. His notion and reasoning was what landed him the leading role in the case. Immediately, he disrespectfully dismissed the first detective's rookie claims. He displayed how there existed no basis for it but a mere presumption.

Gram believed, in theory, that all cases were similar because they all had one thing in common — linkage. To him, linkage was the motive, the action, and the desired result bundled together into one. By defining it, he could explain all three. But in this case, he couldn't find that connection and couldn't quite explain why he felt so unsettled about it. He was grateful that the autopsy reports had discredited the homicide-suicide theory. The reports showed that the male had over-dosed at least an hour before the female was hacked down, making it impossible for him to be the perpetrator. Then, after questioning relatives and friends, his figurative findings began to gain a little more life.

Not one of them had ever seen the two together or knew them to have any type of association with one another. However, they all assumed it had been quite possible that her ex might have known him in some kind of way. Gram fixated his mind on the ex being the priority. First, he needed a name besides the alias 'Kero'. Though it would be enough for now.

Closing his eyes, Gram was leaned backwards in the chair, running through a few thoughts, when his phone came to life. Being a reflex, he quickly snatched it from his hip. "Gram here…

"You kidding me," he uttered after a moment of surprise as his partner continued to relate her newest discovery. "Who's the source… Okay, call and get those phone records asap then meet me at City Hall." He ended the call, becoming excited by the information. Things were coming together after all. And it was now begging for him to add the final touches, completing the puzzle once and for all.

———

Wincing slightly from the tingling pain, Ace rubbed over the gashes on his head, thanks to Ariel's famous shaving expertise. She'd vehemently insisted that he shave his cranium, so he wouldn't look so — him. He agreed like an idiot. Somehow, she persuaded him into giving her the opportunity to practice on his head. Damn, he wished Whiteboy was here. He would have been the first test dummy.

Ace should have known it was some *BS* from the jump when he instructed her to wet his hair after she'd unexpectedly grazed off some skin on the side of his head. But this was his love, who he decided to trust! Blood poured, and he almost fainted. She had made more gashes, trying to avoid previous gashes. It ended up a complete catastrophe, leaving him with patches of crimson colored tissue stuck on different spots of his head.

Whiteboy died laughing upon seeing him. Ace couldn't do or say anything besides give him a look that said *fuck you*. Then, he nodded his patched head toward the minivan. Ariel had scooped it from one of her jays. And, nonetheless, it was very perfect for the task at hand since it was beat up and accompanied by tinted windows and something that would be barely noticed.

Ace and Whiteboy laid across the backseats while Ariel drove toward the destination Whiteboy provided. Ace had told him to call Paul and let him know they needed to meet like yesterday. Time was of the essence. Though he hadn't expected Paul to respond so quickly. He wondered if he should appreciate it because they couldn't afford to sit around and waste valuable time. It was of the utmost urgency that they get out of Atlanta and faster than fast.

If anybody he could think of possessed the means of providing the assistance he sought, it was Paul. The man had resources and money which Ace planned on exploiting, seeing as how he'd done them both a big favor at the cost of whatever remained of his life. As he saw it, Paul — the boss — was in debt with him, and he needed a payment. This would be his mindset from this point on.

Ace listened to the roar of the engine since the atmosphere was silent. The raucous melody, somehow, soothed his mind — probably because chaos had become his world.

His eyes were shut. He wanted to free his mental from thoughts about everything which happened, could happen, and would happen. It had been a minute since he'd cleared his head of it all, giving his mind the time and space to drift off into nothingness. Forty minutes later, Ace caught ear of the brakes emitting the irritating squeak as the van slowed. He peeped over the seat and saw that they were approaching a stop sign.

"How far now?" he asked in wonderment.

"We're here..." she told him, hitting the lights as they were instructed to do.

It was dark out, but Ace could tell that they were surrounded by a lot of woods. Very dark woods. The address was right outside of Clayton County, so he wasn't surprised, just thought it would be more 'public' like the first time.

"Say," he began, still slouched between the seats, "you already know what to do when we hop in with them... Ariel, if I'm not back by nine-thirty, go to the spot in Conyers. Don't waste time second guessing. Aight?" He prayed she'd do exactly what he said besides be Ariel.

"Okay, bae. I got you. But you need to promise y'all gone show up." She needed him to. The three of them were all they had right now, and she wasn't willing to just let them disappear without her taking the initiative to find them both.

"We promise," Whiteboy uttered, obviously tired of the same old worrying shit. He didn't give a fuck if shit got crazy this time with these people. He was determined they would leave one way or another.

The headlights from another vehicle lit up the interior of their van. It was time.

"I love you, Ace… and Whiteboy." Ariel smiled a little, glancing back at them both.

"I love you, Ma." Ace smirked, stroking her face passionately, wanting to give her a kiss, but he thought better of it to wait to later.

"I love you too, Ariel," said Whiteboy, sliding the van door backwards.

Ace blew a kiss in her direction then hopped out into the unknown. Standing there, he heard the van shift into gear and pull away. Then, he turned and saw the man from days ago appear from the same exact van they'd been in the last time.

"Howdy," Whiteboy greeted, bringing a few chuckles from the rest of the henchmen. It wasn't funny to the squad's leader.

"Get the fuck in." He signaled with his automatic rifle. His facial expression let them know he was ready to do whatever — God's or rather Paul's work.

Still at the stop sign, Ace stared him down a moment. The vibe was very different from the last time. Quickly, he realized that they wouldn't be searching them this time. Maybe it was their way of showing them graciousness or having understanding that they had the power. The power. Yet though, they made it evident that the whereabouts were to remain a secret. Without saying a word, the men handed over the same veils they'd worn over their heads the last time.

As the van pulled away, Ace sat in the tight space between the leader and Whiteboy, wondering where they were headed. He knew it wouldn't be the hotel downtown. They were far from that, and he somehow understood they'd be moving a lot farther away. So, he tried to relax on the hard steel as he let his mind drift off like it had done a little time ago. The circumstances, at the moment, was making that difficult to do.

Ace didn't realize he'd nodded off until Whiteboy's voice said loudly, "Ace… Ace…"

"Yeah…" he flatly returned, asking himself, *Why in the hell is it so dark?* Then, he remembered where he was and what was on his head.

"Nigga, take that shit off your head," growled Whiteboy.

"We here?" Ace said while snatching the cloth away. He had to shield his eyes from the interior's bright light.

"Damn, nigga, I thought you had suffocated under that hot mutha-fucka." Whiteboy chuckled along with one of the goons next to him.

"Well, nigga, why the hell didn't you snatch it off? Stupid," Ace muttered, stepping from the van. Instinctively, he gazed around the scenery, stretching and releasing a deep yawn. He couldn't believe he'd fallen asleep at a time like this. He had tripped out then. Ace noticed everything around them was drenched in blackness — well, everything which surrounded the building which was lit up on the inside. The place looked like some type of storage warehouse. He really couldn't tell though; the darkness had obscured some of its phys-ical features.

Moving along, the men escorted them to the inside of the building which possessed the aroma of feces and wet dogs. There were huge shelves that ran about the building's center, but nothing was on them. Then, there were a few forklifts discarded throughout the place. From the looks of it, they hadn't been used in years. On the far end sat a small office, their destination. Within it was an individual behind a desk, talking on the phone.

Paul, Ace realized as they moved closer to it. What an unusual place to meet such a classy businessman.

"Well, well… What a predicament you boys have gotten yourselves into." Paul smiled, placing the receiver down as they stepped in.

"Tell me about it," Ace returned as if it was borderline nothing. He refused to let Paul see him sweating from the pressure.

"Tell you about it? No, how about you tell me since I'm the one doing the fucking guessing about what actually happened," he snapped yet did so calmly, keeping his stare directly on Ace.

Ace wanted to laugh. He had a problem, and he wasn't the one with his picture on every news channel in America. "You know what happened, just like you know everything else, Mr. Paul."

Paul opened his mouth, but nothing fell out. Ace smirked, realizing he needed a moment or two to calculate the amount of information Stacey had possessed. And how much she'd be willing to give if her life depended on it. Paul looked at him a second more, tapping a pen against his bottom lip. Then, he finally let his lips crease back into a smile. "What exactly did she tell you?"

"I don't think it matters at this point. We need help," Ace stated matter-of-factly.

"Help?" Paul seemed as if the word was foreign to him. "Ace, young man, I think you missed my insinuation in our first meeting. I'm not a man that lends helping hands," he said, gesturing with his hands. "I barter. Exchanging considerations in return for considerations. Something for nothing — no. If you want a freebie, I advise you to go to the Salvation Army."

Ace angrily gritted his teeth, wanting to send him somewhere to get some salvation, which was no place on Earth. "I wasn't asking, Paul. You're aware of the situation, like I am, and by me understanding your predicament that puts *us*," he spoke with emphasis, "both in a position to barter. Exchange a consideration for a consideration, as you put it."

Paul leaned back in his chair, taking a deep breath while clasping his hands across his stomach. "Ace, clearly you're out of your league and definitely out of your mind to think that you're in any position to be negotiating…"

"Might be," Ace quickly cut in. "Think about this… me and another person — who's not here — knows about Mr. Gus and his son, Enzo, and about all the mishaps that, if they were to reach Mr. Gus' ears, your position would instantly be similar to ours. Or possibly a little worse, seeing how your people don't play by rules besides their own. So, how about we come to some type of agreement to make sure everyone walks away from this entire mess without a scratch?"

Paul studied him closely, searching for a hint of bluffing, but there was nothing other than the cold seriousness in his eyes. Having played some of the best Poker players, Paul, if anybody, could sense when a bluff or a trick was in the midst. Though tonight, inside of his warehouse office, he'd caught nothing besides the dead stench of the lifeless building lingering in the atmosphere.

After allowing close to a minute and a half for his words to settle on him, Ace felt that he had him exactly where he wanted him and saw no logical reason in continuing to waste time that could be put to good use. "So, what are we doing or going to do?" he asked, careful to keep his demeanor plain. The smallest slip would lead them into their demise and most likely a burial somewhere within this building. Ace had already figured that this had been the reason for a meeting in such an eroding location. Every aspect of the place said it swallowed up way more bodies than he'd slapped up under his belt.

"Well, since you seem to be in *the know*, you tell me. And please don't be reckless or I'll be forced to take my chances," Paul returned, smiling menacingly. Just the thought of Ace having such leverage rubbed him in the most irritating way.

"We going to finish what was started, but we need a way out of town and some financial backing…"

"How would you finish it out of town when the ones in mind are in town?" Paul asked curiously.

Ace smirked at this. "Not all of 'em… Especially not the one in possession of Enzo's treasure."

Paul leaned over the desk, interested. "And she told you this? How you know it's not bullshit?"

Ace stared at him, fully aware that his next words would be a major detail overlooked. "Would a pregnant female, determined to save her life and her unborn child's life, bullshit with a gun to her head?"

Paul couldn't keep his smile from spreading broader across his face. "No, I don't suppose she would. So, where is it!?" His expression now said he was desperate to know.

But Ace wasn't prepared to disclose that pertinent information. This was his only leverage, and if he gave it to him, he might as well personally sign their death certificates. "Somewhere in here…" Ace grinned, tapping his index against his temple.

"Sure it is. However, I think I'm more than obligated to the information since I'll have to provide the means of retrieving it."

"Maybe, but I don't trust the outcome once it's told," Ace cajoled, giving a smirk.

"Yet you want me to believe you and solely trust that you two would locate and return it?"

"Return *half* of it." Ace knew it was best to put it all on the table. This would get to the crux of the situation and how it was to play out. He didn't have time for the sneaky fuckery game, even though he had other things in mind.

Paul said nothing, only let out a small chuckle while straightening his tie.

Ace wasn't finished. "And just in case I do decide to run off with it, at least you'll still have your life." He decided to play around a little since the ball was in his court.

"Ace…" Paul began to loosen his tie and a few buttons on his shirt. "In my way of life, a man's life is not valued because of who he is but because of what he does. Mr. Gus, as you call him, is not a man that mourns or grieves. You can almost consider him immune to human emotions. If Enzo was still alive and Gus had any type of knowledge of what was occurring at the time, he would have had Enzo's head cut off and mounted to his fucking living room wall. Like hunters do to their catch. Make no mistake, this guy is one of the most ruthless people you'd ever run across. He makes Hitler look like a freaking high priest. He is not a person to fuck with." He let out a deep breath. "He wants his diamonds." Paul took another brief pause, clasping his hands down on the desk.

"Now you're in and not because I want you to be. He has eyes everywhere. He knows all. So, let's get back what's his — the money is up for grabs. But those stones, he-will-not-go-without. You understand?"

Ace nodded his head in understanding.

"I'll send one guy with you to get the job done. Then we part ways," Paul assured him, gesturing with his hands.

"That's not good enough…" Ace responded flatly. His situation was a lot more difficult than that.

"Really? I do not see how. You give me the diamonds, you keep the money, and we part ways. How fucking hard is it?" Paul spit out, letting a tad of irritation ride the wave of his voice.

"Even with the money, how far exactly do you think we'd make it? It won't be worth it." He had to chuckle. "Shid, El Chapo money reaches the billions, and he still got caught."

It didn't take a rocket scientist to understand what he was implying, and Paul knew he'd been right to think of it that way. However, that was his problem, but the more he mused over it, the more he realized that Ace's problem could become his. Too many knots would be left untied, which might end up being a detriment.

"We'll work out something when we reach that fork in the road. Alright?" he said, offering the best assurance he could with a smile. He got up, extending his hand toward Ace.

Ace stood and gripped his hand. Now, he was fully aware of how it would end. He needed time to think and only agreed to allow himself some time to do exactly that. Those Mafia dudes were clever, but like every street nigga knew, that shit was no match for the games street niggas were capable of producing, especially when it came to trying to win all the way around the board. And if those muthafuckas didn't know, they definitely were about to find out.

"Aight. We got to grab some shit from our hotel rooms, then we bout to get it." Ace glanced at Whiteboy. Obviously, he had the same thing on his mind. The acknowledgement caused them both to smile.

"Good… Be sure to send my best regards to the absconder in the best possible manner." Paul looked as though he had something else on his mind yet said nothing. He nodded his head toward the guy standing near of them. "Tommy here will be the one traveling with you. So please get well acquainted."

Ace craned his neck, seeing the one who'd been sitting next to Whiteboy when he'd awakened. His expression was one of astonishment. Before stepping out, Ace turned around. "Do you gotta car we can use to make this a little faster? We have a few things to secure as well." Paul couldn't hide his suspicion.

"A car?"

"Yeah. We got a couple of possessions that don't need to be left in the wrong hands, you know."

"Sure, I'll have the guys to take you to one, just be sure to return it. Hate to go through the locating nonsense. It's a headache." He'd spoken it as if it was more of a warning than a mere concern. And Ace took it that he wasn't actually referring to a car. He smiled and stepped out.

———

Minutes Later

PAUL SLOUCHED BACK into his chair, staring at the individual who'd stayed in the office after the entourage left. He smiled that menacing smile. "It seems our little friend has been lying and playing his cards right..." He glanced at his fingers now as if there existed some foul vermin beneath his nails.

The room went silent for a moment. then Paul spoke again. "Bring him in, as they like to say, would you?" Without a syllable being uttered, the man pivoted around and exited, ready to execute his father's wishes.

———

AFTER TAKING damn near thirty minutes to convince Paul's men that they were returning and didn't need Tommy to ride shotgun with them, Ace and Whiteboy were finally allowed the green light to leave by themselves. Well, that was after a call had been placed to Paul, who nonetheless gave the okay.

While Ace drove, he laughed, explaining to Whiteboy why he had bluffed Paul into believing that someone else knew the business. He understood that this was the only safeguard he had. That bluff alone firmly established that they were in a race against time. Anything less wouldn't have been nearly enough to achieve what they had accomplished.

That was why he had conjured it beforehand. Paul had brought them out there for a specific purpose and had every intention of witnessing their execution. But brains and good game had saved their lives. They laughed and made a few jokes about it then let the conversation turn serious. He couldn't think this one out by himself. "Say right, what you think about all of this shit?" questioned Ace, needing his best friend's input and outlook on the entire situation.

"Shid…" Whiteboy began nonchalantly. "On some real shit, I think that once they get what they want, they gone slump us right then and there."

"Damn, we think too much alike," Ace responded with a chuckle. "Nigga ain't going out like that. We need to figure out the best way to do this shit and fast. And leave with them diamonds. I mean, the few mills a be a good look, but aye, boy, them muthafucking diamonds gone be a real ticket."

"I thought you said you know how much they were worth?"

"Nah, I don't. But Stacey said they were worth more than enough to be straight a lifetime and another one. And now, I believe her. Why would this Gus dude be going through all the trouble to get them back? Nigga, you heard Paul say he would kill his own son, basically, for them." Ace smiled, shaking his head a little. This game was ruthless. Anybody could get it.

"True…" Whiteboy agreed. "And it's quite obvious that this muthafucka loaded wit the bread. Too loaded to be worrying about some small shit."

"Ex-fucking-actly. Then Paul easily said we can keep the money. Nigga, be for real. That's four mill. Who lets a muthafucka keep millions like it's nothing? Them diamonds are worth a lot more than I expected, and there's no way I'ma let an opportunity like this pass. Not after all the shit we've been through. Bra, I'm thinking find this shit, the nig…" His words trailed off into nothing. He just remembered something that hadn't crossed his mind since the last time they'd met with Paul.

Damn. He'd been so caught up in the moment that his mouth had spoken words which were only meant for their ears — words capable of costing them their lives before the business was even handled. He wished he could kick himself in the ass two times.

"What?" Whiteboy asked, noticing his sudden pause.

Ace glanced at him then pointed at his ears, twirling his index finger in the air. It didn't take an expert to comprehend the sign language, and no doubt, Whiteboy understood the lingo.

Ace again shook his head, now understanding Paul's real reason for giving the okay. But he'd done that before they'd parted ways. The extra thirty-minute delay was making perfect sense. The man was smart; he had to admit. He had to be smarter.

"Shid, nigga, we got to get in on this. Fuck the bullshit," Ace said, trying to keep the conversation on track. If Paul was listening, it wouldn't take long for him to realize the secret microphones had been discovered — especially if the topic changed abruptly. Plus, Ace would take pleasure in having a chance to mislead him. He couldn't afford to let that advantage slip through his fingers. This shit was chess, and if you intended to win, you not only had to calculate your next moves but your opponent's as well.

"I'm telling ya… We want in. Why? Cause we muthafucking in," Whiteboy chuckled, catching on quickly.

"Fucking right!"

They rode the next twenty some minutes, babbling about a few things unnecessary and spoke very little about what they actually had in mind. Ace knew they really didn't need a plan when it came to tricking the one called Tommy. A little eye contact and head nodding would nonetheless accomplish that.

That wasn't of much concern. However, outsmarting Paul and Gus presented a challenge beyond the ordinary. They'd have to be exceptionally strategic and careful if they wanted to succeed and survive. Paul had a knack for seeing through deception, a skill Ace admired. If this Gus guy could make Paul piss his pants, that was enough to convince him that Gus wasn't — as Paul had said — someone to fuck with.

It didn't matter though. Niggas had a knack for trying shit. That was how they got ahead in life, and Gus would be no different. *Well, maybe a little*. Ace smiled at the thought. He'd survived in this game by trying shit, and right now, he wanted to see how far it would get them. Only one street motto made sense at this moment — "Go in or go the fuck out."

CHAPTER 7

I WONDER what this ho been doing? Whiteboy thought to himself, pulling the vehicle into the Hampton Inn. Sometime ago, he'd dropped Ace off with Ariel, so they could wrap things up on their end, which would aid in turning their new mission into a success. The entire drive, it had played out in his mental, becoming different scenarios of how it could play out.

Out of all the situations they'd encountered, the current one held the potential of curving their little spree into an end. Maybe this time they'd bitten off more than either one of them could chew. But Whiteboy cared less about that. He'd have to be shown. Well, they would. Ace was the only person he was prepared to die with and for. Ace was the only family he'd known besides the other two who were deceased, thanks to his own hands. They were brothers, and Ace had proved that numerous times, especially when he did his little juvenile stretch, a time when nobody stood by his side but Ace.

Hell, he didn't know how he would have made it through and out if it hadn't been for his brother from another mother. He had never experienced such a situation before and was more than grateful for all of it. Circumstances, nonetheless, instilled principles within him that he'd hold high and cherish until his last breath. And one time while making salat, Whiteboy thanked Allah for blessing him with them.

Glancing around, he watched a few hotel guests go into their rooms, and a few leave the premises. The scenery became vacant. Quickly, he stepped from the vehicle, pacing with a purpose. His eyes swept back-and-forth continuously, like he was some kind of paranoid-schizophrenic. Whiteboy's hand clutched tightly around the pistol. He was ready for anything if need be.

Finally, he reached room 312. Whiteboy swept over the area again before removing the key card from his pocket. Then, as silently as possible, he turned the knob a little with his ear pressed against the door. Nothing was heard besides the sounds from the TV, which had been typical considering who was on the other side of the door. He eased in.

"Hey, White…" Michelle thirstily greeted, a little too excited by his reappearance.

His eyebrows furrowed as he said, "What up?" nonchalantly then brushed past her. Heading straight for the bathroom, he switched on the light to inspect. All was well. He reversed!

"Why you got to do all that? Ain't nobody here but me and this fat pussy." She smiled seductively as he knelt down to check under the bed.

"There's nothing like being cautious." He got up, gazing down on her. He was definitely in need of another shot of that fat pussy before they parted ways.

"Mhmm…" Michelle now crawled over toward him, obviously feeling his vibe. "There's nothing like being horny." She bit down on her bottom lip sexually, wasting no time in letting her hands find his belt buckle.

"Sometimes…" Whiteboy stroked her hair, ready to feel the inside of her throat. That instrument was the sole reason behind him bothering to fuck with her in the first place. She was capable of being a freak any time of the day, any place, and a nigga never had to ask for that side of her with his mouth. The eyes spoke a language which she more than understood. But then again, she chased the dick like niggas chased pussy — an all-out nymph.

She giggled at his comment. "Most of the time for me." Tugging, Michelle pulled his jeans and boxers to his knees, exposing his half-erect manhood.

Whiteboy stared down at her, removing the gun from the hoodie's pocket. He then aimed it at her temple.

"Wh…" she gasped, playing as if she'd been startled. Yet the sight of it, along with its target, did all but scare her. Her pussy got hotter and more wet off of shit like this. She was tempted to ask for him to smack her a little bit, though she knew from a previous experience that he wasn't down for that type of kinky shit. "So, you gone kill me, Daddy?"

"Nah, only that mouth. Now suck this dick for real," he told her, already fully aware that any form of aggressive shit was right up her alley, a major turn on to her.

Lifting him, she proceeded in slowly kissing the head then let it slip between her soft lips, keeping her eyes locked on his. He knew this was her way of insinuating that he get a little rougher.

He glared. "Bitch, stop playing and suck that shit," he snarled, pressing the barrel harder against her temple. Gripping the back of her skull with his free hand, he forced all of him into her esophagus.

"Gww!" she gagged awfully as saliva spewed out the edges of her mouth, gushing more and more with each thrust. He couldn't let up or control himself. It was feeling too good for him to call it quits so early, so he continued to pound her throat harder and harder. He had to admit that their freaky ass escapades were wild. But nonetheless, it always, quite strangely, got the job done.

Shoving his shaft deep one last time, he pulled out slowly after hearing the sounds people emitted when they were about to throw up resonate from her windpipe. He damn sure didn't need her to do that.

Clumps of spit bobbed their way down her chin and off to the fabric of the bed while she held her mouth open to catch her breath. However, the way her saliva covered lips creased into a smile made him think she was dying for more. *This ho crazy*, he thought, ready to give her another thrusting. "Take that shit off," he growled, removing the thermal hoodie he was wearing along with the rest of his clothing.

When his shirt dropped, something vital came to mind. "Damn, I'm tripping," he muttered, almost under his breath. Whiteboy had been so caught up in the moment that he'd forgotten the main reason he'd returned.

Angrily, he quickly moved over to the dresser then tilted it forward.

"What?" Michelle questioned, kicking her thong across the room. She was too thirsty for this moment. This had been the roughest he'd gotten, period. Michelle had no idea of what had leaped into him, but damn, she was glad. Just the thought made her pussy pulsate.

Whiteboy said nothing while he reached under, dragging out a small tool kit.

"Please, baby, let's finish this!" she begged, watching him move across the room.

Irritated, he barked, "Bitch, shut the fuck up and chill." Somehow, he knew she would still find his seriousness to be enticing. Fixating the small bit piece onto the bolt, Whiteboy began unscrewing the screws from the hotel vent. This was the securest place he could think of in the small room. And seeing as how Ace had lucked out on his share, he understood they would have to rely on his.

"White, what you doing?" she questioned suspiciously, wondering what exactly caused his undivided attention to be on the ventilator when her vagina needed a serious plumbing. But on the other hand, if it was currency that he'd secretly hidden, she'd be sure to keep that in mind when the time came. Sure, the rough sex was her thang, but nothing made her pussy cum the way money did. That had been her true obsession and her purpose tonight.

"Man, shut up," he uttered over his shoulder, removing the very last screw. Removing its cover, Whiteboy stuck his arm in without hesitation, staring at Michelle, who slowly stroked two fingers in and out of herself. *This ho dumb freaked out.* He smiled. His penis jerked upwards, wishing it had been her fingers.

Straining farther, he finally exhaled, "Gotcha!", a few seconds later. His arm came out covered with streaks of dust, carrying a small duffle bag in tow. Whiteboy slapped the bag a few times, knocking away gray dust, then he sat at the table and unzipped it to check its valued contents. He knew from the jump that it hadn't been touched. But it was better to be safe than sorry.

"What's that?" Watching him had caused her to halt her tease show and hop from the bed. Curiosity always had its way with women.

He smiled, waiting to see her eyes moon. It wasn't every day a bitch saw this many diamonds outside of a jewelry store. "This is Baby's jewelry box — or bag." He chuckled, tilting the tote bag toward her. Instantly, Michelle's retinas turned into headlights.

"Oh, my God… where did…"

Whiteboy cut her nosey ass off. "Don't worry bout all that. Just be grateful." Removing a few pieces, he laid them on the table. "This is for you… preciate you holding the fort down while a nigga did his business."

"For real?" she asked, elated, shocked, and everything else which ran along those lines. She hugged him like a child did their parents on Christmas day.

"Man, calm the fuck down." He tried to sound vexed, but he actually enjoyed her reaction. "You know you owe me now, right?" Seductively, he squeezed her ass with both hands, ready to bust one before they parted ways, which she wasn't aware of at the moment.

"I do, Daddy…" she teased, thinking only if she could suck every part of him.

His dick became hard. Smiling, he glanced down at the floor, eyes locating the object that was bound to make her sex him like she'd never done before. And he had every intention of using it as an accelerator.

Taking him into her palm, she pressed and rubbed it between her pussy lips, wanting him to feel how hot and moist she'd become. *Yeah, it's definitely about to go down*, he began to think, standing as she fell spread eagle across the bed.

Snatching up the Ruger, Whiteboy stared at the lustrous exhibit before she twirled onto all fours, lying her head against the mattress as she spread her legs a little wider, swaying her round bottom from side to side. Only if she'd been another girl, he might have dropped down and ate her from the back. But this was Michelle, the top action of all actioners. Positioning himself, he rubbed the pistol against her clit, causing her to jump a little bit due to the coldness of the steel.

"Sss… oh, damn…" She moaned sexually as he forced it in some.

"You like that shit, bitch?" He tugged her hair hard enough to lift her entire upper body. He wanted to laugh because he was liking this a little too much.

"Yes, Daddy, I love it…" Her moan became deeper. "Make this bitch feel you."

She dumb sick with it. He smirked, launching the barrel a little into her womb. Michelle's body shivered, and her hum vibrated louder. He wondered how pleasurable she'd think this moment was if he let the muthafucka go off in her. That would be a sight to see.

Seconds later, he eased it out. "Clean this," he demanded, wanting to see how far she was willing to go. He wouldn't be surprised, fucking with her.

She pivoted halfway. "Please don't make me…"

"Bitch!" he snapped, cocking his hand in the air as if he was on the verge of knocking her ass out with the pistol. They both burst out laughing. He tried his best to hold it in, but he sounded too stupid to himself.

"Okay, damn…" She had to laugh again before letting the muzzle find her mouth.

Now this ho hard. He watched amusingly as she licked and sucked away her own juices like it wasn't even steel. Finishing, Michelle planted one final kiss at the tip then reached back for the real smoking gun. "Cut the lights off and come dig in this wet pussy with that real shooter."

He loved the way she made that sound. Whiteboy rubbed his manhood up between her ass cheeks a few times. He was going to miss her. Throwing her forward, he moved to the light switch speedily. Then, an odd feeling shot through his body like a lightning bolt, causing his gait to instantly cease. One eyebrow rose as he slowly craned his neck. One finger found the switch.

Michelle was halfway off the bed, displaying an expression that spoke of a thousand words yet not one that related to sex.

Boom! Boom! Boom! Boom!

As if on cue, the gunfire resounded, launching bullets through the door and windows, causing Whiteboy to accidentally knock the switch down as he scattered across the floor in retreat. Darkness filled the room while Whiteboy scrambled for cover at the side of the bed. Michelle screamed like a mad woman, balling herself up on the other side of the mattress.

"Fuck!" he yelled, experiencing the intense burning digging deeper into the flesh of his side. He couldn't register actually where he'd been hit, but it felt like he'd gotten shot a multitude of times. It was as if his body was on fire.

"Fuck nig…" he growled, sticking the pistol over the bed, shooting aimlessly in the direction of the door. He hoped to at least make them back up. The way they were blasting made it seem as if they'd been attempting to knock the entire damn room off.

Still, Michelle screamed frantically from somewhere on the other side of the bed. Right now, he gave two fucks about her because, at the moment, niggas on the other side of the door were letting off like only one thing had been on their minds. Killing some shit.

"Shit…" he moaned. The agonizing pain made its way through his shoulder, forcing him to pull back his weapon. The gun had fallen right on him, which he didn't waste any time in gripping it with his other hand. Hell, at a time like this, he would use his feet if it came down to it. Inhaling deep breaths, he laid still a few moments, shutting his eyes to block out some of the pain and to keep from panicking. The pain was more than overwhelming, and Whiteboy knew if he intended on making it out alive — if that was possible — he'd have to keep a leveled head to make his next shots count. "Fuc…" he huffed, trying to ignore the ache, nonetheless finding it hard too. Michelle's elongated scream wasn't helping either. He found himself wondering how long her lungs could last.

Opening his eyes, he stared off into the darkness, then heard the last shot. Whiteboy maneuvered onto his side and listened. He wished he could slug Michelle's ass because she prevented him from fully hearing everything though was grateful she'd turned the noise down some.

The latch clicked.

He understood now that they were determined to see this thing through till the end, whoever they were. "Ain't going out like Scarface. Ain letting no cowards kill me," he whispered to himself, aiming the pistol under the bed. The obscurity of the room made it hard for him to see the door, yet he knew once it opened, some type of light would spring through.

His eyes locked in on where he remembered the door being. Now, he was waiting on his cue. Then it happened exactly as he expected. The door crept slowly open, letting in minute rays of light from bulbs attached to the walkway. Never would he have thought he'd be so dependent and thankful for them.

Without hesitating a second, Whiteboy squeezed the trigger, letting off shots, forcing the feet to retract backwards immediately. Then, the rapid shooting began again. Whiteboy smirked a little, aware that he'd at least hit one of them, if not both, and likewise, he knew not to let up...

Gaining new momentum, he sat up, aiming the Ruger over the bed, firing two more shots toward the shadow he'd caught a microsecond glimpse of. Using the comforter as leverage, he pushed himself to his feet, easing slowly over to the door, gun extended, keeping his head low. He resembled special ops.

Michelle continued to scream from the corner as he reached one side of the door, peering out.

"Muthafucka," he sneered, glaring at the guy in all black who inched his way sluggishly along the rail. His gun dangled in one hand by his side. Whiteboy was sure that he'd severely wounded his attacker.

"Say!" he barked, shooting him in the back.

"Agh! Shh..." the guy cried out in pain, discarding the weapon. His upper torso bent over the rail like he was attempting to go over it.

Slouching over to him, Whiteboy shot him two more times before growling, "Nigga, who the fuck sent you?"

The man moaned out in distress, taking his first step down the first flight of stairs. "Mon… plea…"

His pleas infuriated Whiteboy even more. At this point, he cared less about who sent him. He wanted death and kept in mind that the police were most likely on the way. Keeping the marker on his target, he moved closer, taking aim directly at his cranium. He squeezed, sending a bullet through the back of his skull.

Before he could watch the body tumble down the stairs, Whiteboy pivoted, quickly heading back for the room.

"Oh, my God! Oh, my…" Michelle cried, careening from the threshold.

He stared at her. What was he to say or do besides that of placing the marker on her, launching two hot ones into her face? Throughout his life, Whiteboy had been called a lot of things — all type of shit. More shit than he could remember. However, being naïve or obtuse wasn't one of them. He was positive that nobody was good enough to peep where he laid low. And this ho had resided here for three days now. So, it didn't take a genius to put two and two together about the entire occurrence. If he was wrong, then it was what it was.

————

"DAMN, I'MA MISS THIS…" Ace breathed heavily after catching one of the best nuts that was much needed. He gazed at Ariel, who was huffing as hard as he'd been, digging her teeth into her bottom lip. She was sexily over exhausted. Ace admired the sight of her like this. There could be nothing sexier. Perspiration streaked wildly over their bodies as he continued to slowly stroke in and out of her, not wanting to leave this position. Her insides felt like Heaven, and he wanted to stay eternally.

She was picture perfect, beautiful, and luscious. He couldn't resist tasting the inside of her mouth. He kissed her passionately while she gripped, tugging on the back of his head.

Ace quickly realized what she had in mind. They both knew this moment would be short lived and postponed until the chance presented itself again. And there was no telling when that would be. He pulled backward, wanting another look to memorize. Then, his phone blared to life.

This nigga always know when to interrupt. Ace chuckled to himself, moving from on top of her. "Yo, nigga, you… Hold up. What?" Ace's mood abruptly changed. Panic rode his voice. He sprang from the bed, alarming Ariel. Something was definitely wrong.

"Shawty, where you at?" he asked, stepping quickly into his pants, struggling to get them on. "Fuck. Fuck… Man, I'm on my way."

Out of all the times she'd witnessed reactions from him, never had her eyes laid on the person before her. "What's wrong?" she finally questioned, partly amazed by how fast he was moving.

This had been the only time he'd slowed his movements. "Man, they got White." Tears piled up in the web of his eyes. Reality was setting in harder.

"Nooo…" she screeched. Tears instantly tracked down her cheeks.

Snatching up the choppa, Ace yanked the slide backwards, loading an .223 round into the chamber. This was war. He grabbed the .45 from the nightstand, shoving it down into his pants. Before Ariel could even insist that she ride with him, he had already disappeared beyond the threshold. She wasn't offended or mad in the least because she knew there was nothing more his ears would have heard.

"These muthafucking niggas done shot my nigga," Ace repeated over and over to himself as he maneuvered the car through traffic recklessly, not caring whose way he got in. Nothing or nobody would stop him, and if any one attempted to, they'd get unloaded on as if they were the ones responsible for shooting his brother. And the police weren't excluded. They were at the top of his list.

At this point, it was him against the world. His best friend had been gunned down, the only person on this planet who'd give anything to be by his side, had taken bullets that were meant for him, and he wasn't even there to take them with him. With each passing moment, the hurt dug deeper into his core due to the simple fact that he'd been in some pussy while Whiteboy was out there fighting for his life.

What the fuck was he thinking? Shit was hitting the fan in a major way, and all he could think about was indulging in pleasure. He should have been trying to safeguard their future in some way. What the fuck was wrong with him? Out of everything he should have done or been doing, why would he allow his dick head to mislead him into thinking he actually possessed a minute or two for pussy?

His life had gone from bitter to shit and was becoming shittier by the day. Now looking at the new circumstances, his future for damn sure didn't seem to be getting any sweeter. Yet he had the nerve to squeeze in a little fun time before what he comprehended as the *real shit* kicked into play. He'd tripped the fuck out, to the highest extent, and was about to pay dearly for it, especially if he couldn't reach Whiteboy, his best friend, his brother, in time.

Ace thought things were grimy before, but now, it seemed as if the game was about to prove once again that he had seen nothing. Continuously, it showed there existed no heart and definitely no sort of favoritism. The game appropriated no feelings, so it cared less about who you were or what you acquired. The moment you slept on it would be the moment it caught you by surprise, knocking you on your ass, daring you to get back up. And if you did, it would lay low in the shadows lurking, waiting to deliver an even harder blow the next time.

There were no rules besides its very own. It didn't deal in fairness, and it possessed no traits of sympathy or remorse. It ate at the soul relentlessly until you were fully devoured. Then, you were trapped — like a caged animal with no outs. Only the infinite in. *When you're in, you're in, and there's nothing that could change that.*

Ace smashed down on the accelerator harder, swerving around a few stagnant vehicles and people who were trying to get out of his way. He was only a short distance away from the hotel Whiteboy had been staying in. He hadn't even gotten close up to it and could see the blue lights flashing, illuminating the hotel's parking lot and the surrounding environment. A few vehicles ceased their movement to get a good look at the scene that appeared to be the presence of the entire Dekalb County force.

Switching to the left lane, Ace eased the rental into a creep, eyeing what he could. The area was crowded with uniforms moving quickly about in all types of directions. He stared, seeing that the third floor was getting all the attention. He didn't have to guess why. Out on the walkway were a few cops standing around, glancing downward, inspecting something near the stairway. The scenery was telling him what he felt but nothing he intended on believing.

Ace prayed it wasn't White. He mentioned he'd been shot, though not how bad he'd been injured. Bringing the car to a stop, he locked in on the room, which police were walking in and out of. Evidently, something of importance laid within the room.

"Fuck!" Ace snarled, punching the steering wheel as he watched a team of medics rush toward the room with their bags in tow. He didn't know if that was a good sign or a bad one. Whoever was inside seemed to be in desperate need of medical attention, and if it was White, he'd remained alive. At the same time, it would still be bad. They were the nation's most wanted.

Ace eyed the room closely in hopes of catching sight of him to be sure. That wouldn't happen though. The bright rays from a flashlight shined onto his face. His heart skipped a beat by the surprise. His hand stealthily made its way to the assault rifle, which slanted downward from the console to the floorboard. At this current moment, he was prepared for whatever, and he refused to go out without a fight. There was nothing to lose.

His jaw clenched tightly, and his eyes landed on the officer who continued aiming the light at his face. But just as quickly, the cop waved it back-and-forth, signaling for him to keep it moving. He wasn't as much relieved as he was grateful for directing instead of the *got him* shit. No doubt it would have been a lose-lose. How in the world would he beat so many alert guns? It was too impossible, he knew. Yet his intention wasn't to be a victor, only a murderer.

Easing his foot off the gas pedal, he slowly inched the car away. Ace drove on, glaring at the officers before stealing one last look at the scene. *Damn, how in the fuck am I supposed to get Whiteboy out of this shit, which I'm the sole reason for?* he wondered, whipping the rental down the street and around the first corner.

This entire mess was a catastrophe, one he had the slightest idea of how to fix. Now, he was by himself again, like he'd been long ago, with nothing more than a gun in his hand and a wild future ahead of him, exactly like long ago. But this time, there wasn't a *Black*, who would pull up to guide, to teach — to use and to kick.

Ace was a grown man at this point and had to make his own decisions because nobody would be able to do that. Hell, who knew what was best for him besides him? He needed time to think. Pulling the car to the curb, he parked. His head fell back against the headrest. Thoughts flooded his mind. He wished he could wash it all away and start it all over from the beginning — all of it, all the way back to that night at the kitchen table down to the first word that started it. He wished he could have started another conversation with Missy instead of the one which transpired. She tried to warn him, but he failed to take heed.

Ace now wanted to apologize and tell her she was right. Tell her that every word she'd ever spoken to him was nothing but the truth. She had been a lot more advanced than him at the street shit, and it took him years to realize it. How incoherent he'd been. If he could take back all that occurred when he first met Whiteboy, maybe he wouldn't have gone through all that he had. Maybe his life would have turned out a little different than it was now. Maybe he'd be somewhere else instead of being surrounded by officers who wanted his head.

A tear treaded down his cheek as he picked up the half of blunt and lighter. He inhaled, hoping the loud would ease his mind.

Fuck! He hated life right now and wished it would all end. Putting the weed in his other hand, Ace removed the gun from his pants pocket. He cocked it back, launching one into the head. His eyes locked on the instrument. It was the thing he'd chosen to live by and die by. It had protected and killed for him faithfully. He wondered if it was capable of doing it one last time as it had done all those other times.

Placing the muzzle against the side of his temple, he fancied about the end result of the mechanism rushing through the wall of his skull, finishing it once and for all.

Wouldn't that be going out like a coward, running away from his enemies without even making an attempt to at least face and conquer it? Nah, this couldn't be the Ace who made a name in the streets as being one of the most dangerous niggas a nigga could bump heads with. He'd been more ruthless in murdering people and not one time ever thought about backing down from any person or anything — let alone running from a situation by killing himself.

If only Black could see him now, he'd be laughing disgustedly at the piece of shit he created. Ace's index finger caressed the trigger. Just the thought of Black infuriated him more — to the point that he was hoping he'd see him to repay him for all the damage. He knew he'd end up in the same place he had.

He held his breath, ready to meet his maker, letting his finger become one with the trigger. Everything at this moment would be by his leave.

"Sorry," he muttered through trembling lips, praying they would resonate to the ones intended.

Then, his phone began to go off, scaring him, causing his lungs to release the air he held in.

Cause you know I love you, I love you, I love you... The Donell Jones remake of the old Stevie Wonder song played loudly from his pocket. Ace didn't have to look at it to know who was calling. Quickly, he silenced it. He wanted to answer but couldn't. The way he was feeling right now wouldn't allow it. Yet didn't she deserve that much? She'd ended up another sacrificed life that chose to stay down with him no matter how bad the weather got. So, didn't she deserve to be with him? To have him there to wake up to and love?

How selfish was he? Everybody in his immediate circle continuously put him first, and still he refused to place anyone's interests before his very own. How self-serving of him? Why did he find that one thing so hard to do? Why couldn't he sacrifice his own self ambitions for the sake of those — of others?

This flaw alone was the one responsible for most of the situations he suffered, including this new one. Feeling the cold metal against his cranium, he let another tear fall, ashamed of himself. How did he ever bring himself to this stage in life?

The fuck am I doing? He let the gun fall from his head. Another tear streaked his face. Ace attempted to take another drag from the blunt he'd forgotten about but noticed it had gone out. He reached for the lighter. Right when he was about to grab it, something tugged at his peripheral. Ace slowly craned his neck and saw an SUV, which had crept up on the side of him. He really couldn't make out its color or the model it was due to the object protruding from the passenger side window, begging for his undivided attention.

"Fu…" His mouth fell open at the sight of a ghost from the past. Then came the exploding flashes of gunfire. His body turtled after feeling the first piece of lead penetrate his flesh. At this moment, he knew there existed nothing which would intervene between him and the inevitable. He'd been caught down bad.

Seconds later, Ace heard the last shot then the echoes of screeching tires as the SUV sped away. He now laid there, slumped over both seats, holding onto what was left of his life. Never could he have seen this coming and never had he thought that he'd be so ready for death to run its course.

Flashbacks of his life began to replay themselves while the surrounding reality faded slowly into the black.

"Baby, I love you." Sassy smiled with her arms lacing themselves around his neck.

"I know you gon' fix it. You too strong, Ace," Missy said, giving him a stern look.

"My nigga, we good. Ain't shit gonna live if we can't." Whiteboy smirked, snatching back the slide of his 9mm.

"Ace, baby, you got my loyalty and my life." Ariel stared into his eyes.

THE CHAPTER OF FRESHMAN BLACK

A Year Before
Day 1

"AH, FUCK!" He coughed after being thrown under the flickering light pole. His vision was blurred, as though something obscured his sight. The two figures looming over him were mere shadows, their words a garbled mess he couldn't understand. What had happened? He couldn't remember anything beyond who he was and waking up in the midst of being dragged from a vehicle.

Why can't I see? he wondered, panic rising in his chest. What had they done to him? "Fuck..." he grumbled as a third figure stepped into view. Why couldn't he see their faces? The darkened figure in the middle knelt down. His words were nothing more than a jumble of incomprehensible mumbles. Had he gone deaf as well?

Then the figure stood...

He jolted awake, gasping for air. The nurses rushed in, their voices a mix of concern and urgency. One of them hurried out to fetch the doctor. His eyes darted around the room, disoriented, trying to make sense of where he was.

"You're in the hospital," one of the nurses said gently, placing a reassuring hand on his arm. "You've been in a coma for two weeks. You're safe now."

The doctor arrived, examining him with a practiced efficiency. "How are you feeling?" he asked, checking the monitors.

He could only nod, still processing the nightmare and the fact that he'd been in a coma for two weeks. Then everything went black again.

Day 2

The next day, he lay in bed, staring at the ceiling. The room was quiet save for the occasional murmur from the hallway. Two detectives entered, their badges gleaming under the harsh lights. "Mr. Diaz, how are you feeling?" one of them began, flipping open a notebook. "We need to ask you some questions about the night you were shot."

He frowned and wasn't going to summon the memories that still somewhat eluded him. "I… I don't remember what happened," he admitted, frustration evident in his voice.

The second detective leaned in, his expression softening. "You sure there's not anything you can tell us? It will help. You don't remember seeing any faces? Hearing their voices? How about turning your vehicle into the gas station?"

He shook his head, wincing at the pain the movement caused. "No, nothing. Just flashes… shadows."

The detectives exchanged a glance, their disappointment clear. "Alright," the first detective said, closing his notebook. "We'll be back. If you remember anything, no matter how small it is, let us know." As they left, a wave of helplessness washed over him. The memories were there, he knew, just out of reach, like pieces of a puzzle scattered in the dark. He closed his eyes. Desperately, he wished he could penetrate his memory bank and fill in this blank part of his life.

The door clicked shut, and the room fell into silence. He sat motionless, his mind battling itself to retrieve the images that refused to surface. Each fleeting glimpse felt like a cruel tease, fading as soon as it appeared. He rubbed his temples, trying to force the memories forward, but the harder he tried, the more elusive they became.

Day 5

"I'm saying, love, if this heart machine goes off, then you'll come running, right?" he asked, admiring the pretty white girl before him. She reminded him of the porno star, Kelsi Monroe — pretty face and a physique that matched Aphrodite.

"Running? Yes, but only if there's a serious problem, Mr. Diaz." She giggled.

"Okay, I got a serious problem. It's called loneliness, so how about we save you the running and you sit here with me? Every time you leave, my heart aches." His hand clutched onto his hospital gown as if his heart was already beginning to have problems as soon as she stepped toward the threshold.

"So, what am I supposed to do about all my other patients if I'm here tending to your every need?" she asked, her voice dripping with playful seduction. Her eyes traveled slowly down the length of his body, lingering just long enough to make her intentions clear. The way she looked at him, as if undressing him with her gaze, sent a shiver down his spine. She loved this game — the subtle dance of power and temptation. Nothing thrilled her more than the art of a well-placed tease, the promise of something more just out of reach.

"Shid, how many nurses work here again? Let some of them lazy ass girls do their jobs sometime..."

"Wi all do wi jobs, Mr. Diaz." The senior nurse, Mrs. Clarke, walked into the room with her Jamaican accent, clipboard, and her same attitude in tow. She was much older than he preferred his women. But the way she swayed her voluptuous ass from side to side when she walked caused him to think about testing the cougar's water these past few days.

"Good morning, Mrs. Clarke," he greeted, brandishing a fake smile.

"Oh, please. Don'tcha *good morning* mi now after yuh call mi and mi gyal dem lazy."

"Mrs. Clarke, ain't nobody said nothing about your lovely, beautiful self. I said girls which," he leaned over the bedrail some to give her bottom half a good look, "you is very far from." He bit down on his lower lip, trying to look sexy.

"Uh, look at you. I'm jealous," the first nurse said before laughing amusingly.

"Bwoy, please. Mrs. Clarke chew up yuh bony butt and spit yuh out like yesterday trash. Yuh American bwoy don't know nuttin 'bout how to please a real woman. Yuh only know how to play wid toy and be fool-fool," she told him while marking on his chart.

"Tell him again, Mrs. Clarke," the nurse laughed.

Mrs. Clarke's laugh suddenly went dull after her attention steadied on something beyond the door's threshold. Instinctively, Ricardo's retinas darted toward the door frame. At first, he couldn't see what or who Mrs. Clarke had laid eyes upon.

"Good morning, ladies…" For the first time since walking in, the bald headed, white guy turned his gaze on Ricardo. "And gentlemen. How's the injured?"

"And yuh are?" Mrs. Clarke questioned, eyeing the man suspiciously.

"Oh, how rude of me. I'm Special Agent Eric Swift. D.E.A." With that, baldie flashed his credentials for everyone present to see.

Damn. Ricardo stared at the man dressed in casual jeans and a burgundy t-shirt with 'I Kick Ass' printed across the front. He might have doubted that he was a federal agent if he hadn't seen the weapon on his hip. Ricardo began to wonder what the reason for the D.E.A. wanting to see him could possibly be.

The detectives had tried to question him about his injuries and the events of that night. But at the time, he had no answers for them — or for himself. Then, a day ago, small portions of that evening began to replay in his mind. Now, a Drug Enforcement Agency special agent stood in front of him with the words 'serious business' practically written above his head. Ricardo's mind quickly brought back a few moments from the night he was shot. His car had been hit, and for some reason, he started running. Then, somewhere after that, he was dragged out of the back of a vehicle by two people. He still couldn't see their faces. They had dropped him under a bright light, and then someone shot him — once, twice — four times as the doc had told him.

But had there been dope in the car? he asked himself. That was something he couldn't remember, and even if he did, he was certain it wouldn't have been enough for the federal government to get involved. Black had a set of rules in place when it came to moving large amounts of dope, and carrying a load alone in his car was definitely not part of the equation.

"Wi leave yuh two," Mrs. Clarke said, gesturing for the other nurse to follow her out.

"Later, beautiful," Ricardo said to Nurse Crawford, hating that two unwanted and unexpected visitors had ruined what could have been a pleasant morning for both of them.

"Later, you." She smiled, lightly brushing past the agent.

Swift smirked as he smoothly spun around, his eyes tracing the young nurse's figure. "Later, beautiful..." He mocked Ricardo, bringing a giggle from the girl. "With a view like that, someone's clearly been enjoying themselves." His gaze returned to the person he was really there to see. The smirk still lingered on his face.

"Why you here?" Ricardo asked, becoming irritated.

"The same reason you are..." Swift brought his hand up to his face as if he was trying to shield his next words from someone else. "Because of bad fucking luck." He chuckled.

"Listen, man, I've already told the detec..." The agent cut him off.

"Fuck what you told them..." Swift leaned on the bottom bedrail, gazing over Ricardo's blanketed body. His eyes then settled on Ricardo's feet beneath the covers. With a sudden aggression, Swift grabbed a foot.

"Man, what the fuck?!" Ricardo quickly yanked his foot from his grasp. *What type of shit this freaky ass cracker on?!*

"Had to make sure that all of you is still with us." Swift laughed, walking toward the window. "So, Mr. Ricardo Diaz... I'm really trying to figure out where to start exactly." Agent Swift folded his arms across his chest and looked at Ricardo with a raised eyebrow. "Didn't you become Black's right-hand when the unfortunate happened to Mal?"

"Who? Black... Mal? I don't know either of them or anything about being a *right-hand* to anybody but myself," Ricardo told him, knowing better than to even acknowledge knowing them. He wasn't new to this. Police and Feds alike always — first and foremost — searched for a connection in a given matter to start from. Most of the time, if they didn't have that, they'd be lost on all accounts.

Swift stared at him a moment with a mischievous smirk on his face. "Okay," he began like he'd snapped out a brief daydream. "I–I can see where this is going. I'm a cop, and you don't talk to cops..."

"Exactly," Ricardo cut in quickly, confirming that fact.

Swift let out a chuckle as he moved to shut the door. "See, that's the thing. Your perspective on this is all wrong. Yes, I'm a cop — well, a special fucking agent for the United States government." He gripped the bottom of the bed again, causing Ricardo to instinctively pull his feet back. "But here's the thing about being an agent. You have a choice — either be a good, by the book, law-abiding federal enforcement officer or be the most conniving, law breaking, murdering son of a bitch backed by the strong arm of the government." With those last words, his face twisted into a devilish grin, only to shift to an elated expression in an instant.

"But me — Special Agent Swift —_I'm neither. No." Swift walked over and moved the visitor's chair closer to the bed before taking a seat. He leaned back, interlocking his fingers as they rested on his midsection, while his legs crossed as his feet rested on Pee Pee's. "I'm in a little league of my own. You could say I do whatever's necessary to achieve my goals — goals that, might I add, are neither on behalf of the government nor in its best interest. I do what needs to be done for me and mine. I'm pretty sure you can relate to that, right?"

Ricardo didn't say a word, only stared at the psychotic man.

"Well, if you don't, that just means that you suck at handling your *manly* responsibilities," Swift laughed, "which is why I'm here to help..."

"Help? Listen, Special Agent whatever, I don't know what this pose to be about or what you want…"

Swift smiled. "I thought you'd never ask. What I want is to seize a once in a lifetime opportunity. And I want your help to do it."

"My what?" Ricardo couldn't believe that he'd seen the day when a federal agent would have the audacity to ask him — out of all people — for help.

"Uh…" Swift rolled his eyes toward the ceiling before placing them back on Ricardo. "I want your help to seize a once in a lifetime opportunity. Am I speaking fucking Spanish?"

"Man, I can't help you with nothing."

"You can, and you will, my dear friend, Ricardo. You see, while you've been in here for these past two weeks, sleeping comfortably, certain events have transpired that have pushed my goals a little farther from my reach. Events that I'd say are the king's fault."

"And what the hell do that got to do with me? Like *you* said, I've been in here sleeping for two weeks." Ricardo slowly inched his hand toward the nurse's call button. This so-called D.E.A. agent was moving a little too weird for his liking.

"At first, it had nothing to do with Ricardo Diaz, a.k.a. Pee Pee. By the way, why do they call you Pee Pee? Was the name given due to some kind of urine disorder you suffered? I mean, if the name came about during childhood, then I clearly get it. We all had accidental mishaps as kids. But I can't understand why you'd keep the name well into your adult years. Is it be…"

"Man, it's just a fucking nickname my pops started calling me."

"Uh, okay, sorry for asking. Geez," Swift said while lifting both hands defensively. "But anyhow, it seems as if the responsibilities and duties of the king have fallen upon the king's chancellor, which is you."

"What is you talking about?" Ricardo was completely lost. He didn't know any *kings* to be responsible for — nor anything that would make him a chan — whatever he'd called him — for that matter. "You got the wrong person because I don't know any kings."

Swift leaned in, a sly grin spreading across his face. "You may not know any kings, but in our world, there are always people sitting on thrones. And whether you like it or not, you've just been handed the keys to a kingdom. Now, what you choose to do with them… well, that's up to you."

"Bro, I've been in the hosp…"

"Fuck!" Swift huffed, massaging the bridge of his nose as he slouched back into his seat. "Okay, let's try this. Two weeks ago, an anonymous call was made to the Dekalb County police about a shooting and an explosion whereas a burning SUV was found. Police then located a man, presumed dead, lying under a light pole with four bullet holes in him. Good luck and God's grace were both on his side, which is why he's here alive today. Unfortunately, good luck and God's grace wouldn't extend to the king…"

Ricardo curiously stared at him, his mind starting to piece together fragments of memory. The wheels of his memory began to turn, bringing forth something he hadn't thought about since he woke up in the hospital. Flashes of fire, gunshots, and the smell of burning rubber pushed their way to the forefront, unsettling him. He hadn't fully grasped the weight of it all until now, but Swift's words were dragging the details out of the shadows. A cold realization crept up his spine. He had been there — and not there.

"Approximately twenty-eight hours later, Cobb County police would get their own anonymous tip about a shooting. Four deceased persons, along with a 'surviving by a thin thread of fucking life', unconscious male would be found." A new intensity entered Swift's eyes as he continued to give the narrative. "Two of the deceased were females, one of which carried a life, and the other was collateral damage. Then you have the two deceased males…"

Black had mentioned that we would be going to get the work back from Ace and… Ricardo's left eyebrow arched as the brief recollection began to play itself out. He remembered sitting in the room with Black. The tension was high. Ace had taken his shit and some muthafuckas had set it up. *Who had Black said they were though?* Ricardo's mind raced, grasping for the name that had slipped through the cracks of his memory. He knew it was important, but it was just like every other thought, out of reach.

"One of the men was a dear friend of mine. A hard-set guy who was a dedicated patriot and servant to Uncle Sam and all of his apparatus. Twenty-six years in all he'd served the government that had nothing to offer him besides an undercut salary which failed to meet any of his needs. Or any of ours for that matter." Taking a deep breath, Swift stood and walked back into the sun's rays coming through the window. "Then came operation *Lily Bird*, which is what *we* called it." He looked down, examining his fingernails as if he was in deep thought. Swift then smiled, putting his eyes back on Ricardo.

"Operation Lily Bird is a very sensitive topic for me. I won't get into the origins nor the specifics. But this op wasn't just any old mission. There was a very important life at stake, and my friend, after all his long years of service, decided to put his life on the line for a person he considered family. So, one day, him and this person he thought to be family was blessed with an op that would solve all of the problems. I mean everything…" Swift turned around, sitting on the windowsill. Casually, he stuffed both hands into his pockets.

"So, we did the op, and it was a success, except for one mishap and a bad fucking temper — two things that would turn a successful and lucrative operation into a full-scale disaster." Swift smirked, but nothing about it seemed genuine. "And when I say full-scale disaster… Bonds would be broken. Lives shattered. Trust would turn into deceit, and friends would turn into flat out monsters. And so would my friend and myself." With those last words, Swift interlocked his fingers to crack his knuckles, becoming a little intense.

"Sure, I had my own demons to fight, but it could never compare to the battle my friend faced. The weight of betrayal can twist a person, turn them inside out until they're unrecognizable — even to themselves. And that's what happened. It wasn't just about the money or the diamonds. It was about the unraveling of everything we thought we stood for. My friend lost himself in that chaos while I… well, I just learned how to survive it."

Swift's eyes darkened, his voice carrying a mix of regret and cold acceptance. "You see, my friend had ties. Deep ties — not just with street thugs but with the Mafia. He thought he could use them to his advantage. Which is how he met the king — Black."

Black... It was now all coming back to Ricardo like the rerun of an old movie.

Swift's voice lowered as if he were revealing a dark secret. "Black wasn't your run-of-the-mill kingpin. He had written the rules for this game, using them to build his empire on fear, blood, and control. My friend thought he could rise to the top by playing both sides, but he was a fool. See, as you know, you don't just meet Black. Black meets you, and once you're in, he owns you."

Swift paused, letting the name hang in the air. "And as you know, Black was something else, someone who had built his empire on blood and fear. My friend, blinded by ambition and desperation, thought he could use Black. Thought he could rise to the top by playing both sides. But you don't just meet Black, now do you? He chooses you, and if you're not careful, he'll make sure you regret ever stepping into his world."

He cracked his knuckles again, his voice full of intensity. "That's where everything went to hell. One unfortunate introduction and a ton of karma suddenly had the Mafia, Black, and the whole damn city aiming at our heads. My friend thought he was a player in the game, but Black was the one writing the rules."

A smirk briefly flickered on Swift's face, but it quickly faded. "But even kings fall. Black had written his final rule without even knowing it..."

"Hold on, hold on..." Ricardo began as he sat up. "What is you saying?"

"The same guy who put four bullets in you, Ricardo, is the same one who shot Black down. One shot — well-placed — and there the king fell."

"Man, get the fuck outta here. Ain't no nigga stupid enough to shoot Black, and Black for damn sure ain't fell."

"Funny, isn't it? The one who thought he was untouchable taken out by something he finally didn't see coming." Swift smiled while biting down on his bottom lip. His knuckles cracked once more as he became gratified by the revelation. "Black thought he could control everything, but in the end, the rules he wrote were used against him."

Ricardo gritted his teeth, his hands clenching tightly onto the bed dress. *Ain't no way Black dead!* The thought echoed in his mind, and disbelief began to mingle with anger. Black was supposed to be untouchable, invincible. The idea that someone had taken him out so easily didn't sit right.

"Yeah, I know what you're thinking," Swift said, watching Ricardo's reaction closely. "But trust me, it's true. Black's dead, and the streets are already shifting — sections are up for grabs, and people are scrambling to fill that void."

Ricardo's jaw tightened. This changed everything. The realization hit him hard, sending a surge of adrenaline through his veins. If Black was really gone, the game was about to get even more treacherous — and personal. Leaving him where exactly?

"A void that belongs to his second in command — which is you," Swift said, forming his hand into a gun, aiming at Ricardo.

Ricardo wanted to snap. His chest tightened as his mind raced. His eyes narrowed, burning with a mix of rage and realization. The special agent was right. With Black dead, the Hand — the throne — was his. He would see it no other way. But it wasn't just about claiming power. It was about his loyalty, his revenge, and him stepping into a role he never imagined would be his. Black had been more than a boss. He was the code Ricardo lived by. Now, without him, everything would be different, and there was no turning back.

Ricardo clenched his fists, struggling to keep his emotions in check. There would be time to think, plot, and take what was rightfully his. But first, there was one thing gnawing at the back of his mind. He needed answers. "What did Black have to do with them diamonds?" His voice came out low and calm, but beneath the surface, a storm was brewing. He wasn't just asking for information. He was preparing.

Swift's eyebrow arched, then his smile returned. "I mentioned diamonds? Well, that was a mistake on my part. You'll have to forgive me. Black had nothing to do with the diamonds and neither do you. So, how about I make it a little simpler? I've already overstayed my welcome. The kingdom has been taken and split amongst some of the king's men. If you want what's reasonably due, my assistance is the only way it's gonna happen. And vice versa, your assistance is a important part to the completion of my goal."

"What the fuck makes you think that I'll help you?"

Swift lifted his balled fist to his mouth and bit down on the skin of his index finger. A few seconds of silence would pass before he spoke. "Uh, let's see…" Within an instant, he'd closed the small distance between the two of them. Before Ricardo could react, Swift had quickly snatched up his arm while wedging his right hand into his throat. Leaning, he pressed his body weight against Ricardo, who attempted to jerk away but couldn't. Futile, Ricardo reached with his left arm. He now realized how weak his body really was.

A few muffled gasps escaped Ricardo's mouth before Swift began to speak lowly. "It takes approximately two minutes for a person to lose consciousness. A minute if the person exerts energy by struggling. And almost three minutes for the mutherfucker to become dead. That leaves you with a little over sixty seconds to save not only yours but also Mario's life."

Ricardo's jaw clenched tighter as he used his shoulders to lift what he could of his upper body from the bed. He hadn't thought about him until his name slipped from the agent's mouth. Mario, his twelve-year-old brother, lived with their mother — the same mother who refused to let Ricardo be a part of either of their lives. The bitterness between him and his mother was a situation of its own, but despite that, he loved his little man to death.

Swift offered a menacing smile. "Thought that would get your attention. You and me have a fate to fulfill, so I think it's best you get your shit together." He released Ricardo and began to adjust his attire.

"I'll kill you before you touch my little brother," Ricardo huffed after a deep breath.

A smirk appeared on Swift's face. "That's the spirit. I'll be watching and will get in touch once you complete the first phase of our little agreement. Take back what belongs to Black, and maybe a few *new* arrangements can be made regarding those stones. But only if you meet expectations." With that, Swift removed a card from his billfold. He extended it but pulled it back once Ricardo hesitantly reached for it. "Don't waste my time." The card flipped from his hand toward Ricardo as he walked out.

Ricardo's hand hovered over the card Swift left behind. His chest rose and fell with steady breaths, but his mind was anything but calm. The weight of the situation weighed heavily on him. Black had died. The thought pierced through him like a sharp blade. Swift had been right about one thing. The Hand was his. No one else's. That throne, that power, everything Black had built... it was now in his lap.

His fingers brushed over the card that felt heavier than it should. Taking the Hand wasn't just about gaining its power though. It was about revenge. It was about payback. Black had taught him that, in this world, loyalty and disloyalty went hand in hand. You couldn't expect to have the former without the latter lurking somewhere in the background. Nor would the ambitions of the latter wait on the former to clear its way, which Swift's words had made evident. The vultures had already circled and landed.

Then, he thought of Mario, his little brother. He hadn't wanted this life for him, but somehow, a threat had dragged him into it. He'd have to step up, for Mario, for Black — for himself. There was no turning back.

Ricardo squeezed the card in his hand, his knuckles whitening. His mind raced through everything Black had said, every lesson he'd drilled into him. This wasn't just about survival. This was now about saving a life and reclaiming what was to be his. He would make everyone who had crossed Black — or dared to rise up against him — pay. Every move had to be calculated — every decision precise. He wasn't just going to hold the Hand — he was going to take back everything they thought it had stolen and more.

He stared down at the card again, what a small piece of his future left in his hands. Swift had placed a challenge in front of him, but Ricardo knew it was much more to it than that. Taking a deep breath,

Ricardo placed the card on the nightstand and reached for the phone. There were people who needed to hear his voice.

Day 16

"Bitch..." Pee Pee grumbled, sprinting toward the four-way intersection. He could feel the burning sensation from a slug launching into his side. His eyes swept over everything in front of him, in search for a quick exit out of this situation.

"Get the truck!" Pee Pee heard someone yell from behind him before a car horn blared. The car had swerved around him, missing his legs by mere inches...

BOOM!!!

His head instinctively ducked as the gunshot rang out behind him. Thinking that was the gunman's final attempt at ending his life, Pee Pee gratefully ran onto the illuminated lot of Phillips 66 where people were scrambling for cover. He could now feel the blood oozing between his fingers as he slowed his run. Quickly, Pee Pee spun around, aiming his pistol, but saw no one in pursuit of him.

"Muthafuc..." he huffed, squeezing the wound in hopes of slowing his blood loss, at least until help showed up, which he knew would be soon. Someone had shot and chased him in front of all types of people, who most likely were afraid and already making calls to the Dekalb County police. Normally, the presence of the police meant a bad situation for him, but tonight, they would be his savior. However, if he didn't find somewhere to get rid of his pistol before they showed up — regardless of how injured he was — it would end badly for him.

Glancing over his shoulder and around in search of his pursuer, Pee Pee saw nothing resembling a threat. Though his moment of relief was brief. The sound of screeching tires caused him to snap his head toward the direction the noise had come from. Damn, it was the SUV that had hit his car from behind. "Fuck!" It was more than clear now that these niggas were intending on finishing what they started.

Pee Pee was in the act of raising the pistol when something slammed into him from behind with such force that it sent him crashing to the ground, and the pistol flew from his hand. "Bitch ass nigga!" was all he heard before a light skinned dude hurriedly turned him over and bashed him in the face with the butt of a gun. The pain shot upward through Pee Pee's nose. His sight instantly blurred from the impact, along with his thoughts of survival. What a turn from worse to straight fucked up this had become. He reached for what he thought to be the man's face. Quickly, his attacker shot him an elbow to his jawbone with a blow to the temple using the gun. This caused Pee Pee's body to go limp.

The driver of the SUV hopped out, and the two men snatched Pee Pee up, throwing him across the backseat of the vehicle. "Go!" the passenger yelled at the driver, pushing Pee Pee's legs over so he could get in.

"Ho ass nigga!" the man growled, striking him two more times. Pee Pee's world slowly went black.

"Shawty, I told you you missed the turn…" Pee Pee stirred awake. The awkward position of his body made him want to adjust, but the sudden memory of how he ended up there froze him in place. His mind raced, replaying everything before it all went black. He hesitated then finally decided to shift his aching body weight. He moved, and his captor tensed.

"Nigga, play wit it," the man snarled, placing the sight of the pistol inches away from his face.

Pee Pee gritted his teeth. They had him down bad, but there was no way in hell he'd just go out without putting up some type of fight. Though what kind of fight would he put up with a bullet in his side that was still burning with pain? Without a second thought, his hand shot upward, grabbing the barrel of the gun.

"Nig…" The two men began struggling for control of the gun. The SUV rocked as they wrestled, then the gun went off with a deafening bang, sending the hollow point through the windshield. Glass sprayed from the windshield, causing the driver to slam down on the brakes, bringing the vehicle to a screeching halt on the shoulder of the road. The sudden stop jerked them all forward. As if a bright idea had come to mind, the captor released one hand from the gun and drove a fist

into Pee Pee's side, right where he'd been shot. Pee Pee gasped as the pain shot through him. Another blow was delivered to his wound, weakening his strong hold on the pistol.

Suddenly, the door his head had been pressed against flew open. "Let it go!" the big driver growled before sending a strong right hook into his face. The punch dazed him, placing him on the threshold of losing consciousness.

"Aye, grab that..." Pee Pee heard the captor say, who was now over him. His eyes were blurred to the point that he could only make out the silhouette of the man's body before his world was engulfed in darkness.

———

*H*IS HEAD FELL *backwards into the dirt, his body trembling with the weight of the inevitable. He opened his eyes, squinting at the harsh fluorescent light shining down from above. How could he know where he was and yet not know where he was? Pee Pee's gaze followed the length of the rays until they rested on a figure holding something out to him. The blurry image began to sharpen with each passing second.*

Now the realization of what was happening set in. A person he had vowed to kill was standing in front of him, and his gift was the barrel of a gun. "Die slow..." The words would not get a chance to settle before three rapid blasts sounded off. He could feel the slugs enter his chest cavity with the last one grazing away the hair and skin from his skull.

"Fuck!!!" Pee Pee screamed from the intense pain. He gripped his head with both hands as he shook himself awake. Quickly, he sat up, wanting to squeeze the pain from his cranium. His eyes opened. The light above was flickering as a mist of dirt blew around his body. His fingers eased along the edge of the fresh wound on his head. How am I still ali...

"How you get caught up like that? Bullshitting around, huh?" Black asked as he took another pull from the Backwood. A cloud of smoke swirled from his mouth and nostrils.

"Man, them nig..." Pee Pee's words trailed off as his eyes dropped

to his bloody hands. Was this real? Or was he — himself — dead? His eyes found the light silhouette of his former mentor, Black. "How?" he now asked, sweeping his eyes around the pitch-black scenery. There was nothing present besides him, the darkness — and the dead.

"How what? How I'm here — or how I died?" Black turned around to face him. His physique was shrouded in darkness, leaving nothing but the red cherry from the cigar to be seen. The light flickered, and Black was within a few feet of him. He knelt down, sliding his fingers across the dirt, as smoke slithered its way out of his mouth. His eyes locked on the living. "Those questions will have their time later. Don't you think that you should be focused on how you're going to get my shit back?"

Pee Pee swallowed hard. "I'm going to get it back."

"Really?" Black chuckled. "How the fuck you gonna do that laid up in here?" Within an instant, Pee Pee was back in the hospital room. Black stood close to the bottom of his bed. After exhaling a lung full of smoke, Black dumped ashes onto the bedspread before moving for the chair. Taking a seat, he crossed his legs as his feet rested on the bed. Exactly like Agent Swift had done. "Tell me?"

Pee Pee sat there a minute, thinking about the best way to verbalize what he had in mind. But he knew there was no perfect way to say anything when it came to Black. He'd read between the lines of any bullshit. So, it was best to just be direct about it. "Shid, I'ma kill whoever I got to to get what's yours..."

"To get what's ours," Black corrected him. Pee Pee stared at his mentor, understanding exactly what he was getting at — and hating that fact.

"I'ma kill the muthafucka that killed you too. I promise, big bra." Pee Pee's voice was cracking as his words set in. He could feel a tear forming in the corner of his eye, but he held it back, refusing to let it fall in front of the man he held in high regard. Black wasn't just a mentor; he was the man Pee Pee had grown to love like a father. Black was the one who taught him about surviving the streets and about what loyalty was.

A flood of memories came to the forefront of his mind, every lesson and every hard-earned piece of respect Black had shown him. He took another hard swallow. The pain was cutting deeper than any wound he'd ever felt. Black had been his anchor, and now he was buried in the dirt somewhere. The tear broke free, trailing down his cheek as the promise he'd made settled into his bones. He would never turn back from it. Pee Pee would make those responsible pay while making sure the streets remembered Black's name — even if it killed him. But didn't he feel already dead?

Black smiled. "I know you is. But first, take back my throne. You heard what that conniving muthafucka, Swift, said. Someone is sitting in our chair, laying claim to everything I built — what we built. How many times have we bled and fought to maintain it? How many of our brothers have died for the kingdom? Just for it to end up in the hands of a new king…"

"He ain't a king." Pee Pee's fists clenched. The weight of Black's words pressed down on his entire body. His chest tightened, rage simmering just beneath the surface. How could someone else call themselves the king? Black had built this empire from the ground up, and now some nigga thought he could step in and take what wasn't his. The thought made Pee Pee's blood boil.

"He ain't did shit to deserve it. None of them did," Pee Pee growled. His voice was low and full of venom. His knuckles turned white as his grip tightened. "Niggas think they can just take what's ours? Fuck no. I ain't letting that happen, period."

Black took another pull from the Backwood. His eyes narrowed. "Do you know what it takes to be a king, Junior?"

Pee Pee could only stare in return because that was terrain he'd never traveled. Of course, he had envisioned himself being the top dog at times — hell, even dreamed about it on numerous occasions. But if he was being all the way a hundred about it, he always saw himself under the wing of his teacher. Black's prowess, he could never match. This understanding now caused him to wonder about if he could really carry the mantle of a king? The streets didn't care about dreams. They cared about power. Respect. Fear. And Pee Pee wasn't sure he possessed all of that just yet.

Black exhaled, smoke curling up toward the ceiling. "It takes more than just wanting it, Pee. You've got to take it. Command it. Being a king ain't about dreaming. It's about making sure everyone knows who you are and making examples of why a muthafucka can't take shit from you. You think you're ready for that? Are you ready to be a king? To be a king is to kill a king."

Pee Pee's heart pounded in his chest. This was his moment, his chance to prove he wasn't just another soldier under Black's empire but someone who could take control of the whole thing. He could feel the pressure in his veins, the weight of the crown looming over his head. "I'm ready," Pee Pee finally said. His voice was steady. It was either now or never.

"Good. A king doesn't just wear the crown. He earns it every damn day." Black smiled proudly before vanishing into thin air. Pee Pee watched until every last particle of guidance dissolved into nothing. He sat there, frozen, with his thoughts being the only things moving. Black was gone, and his empire — his legacy — now rested solely on Pee Pee's shoulders.

BEEP. Beep. Beep…

Pee Pee's eyes fluttered open. The room was cold with a glimpse of the morning sun peeking its way past the curtains. He looked over at the monitors chirping to the beat of his life's pulse. Pushing the cover from his body, he sat upward, wasting no time in removing the IV and heart monitor electrodes from his body. Irritated by the flatline sound coming from the monitor, Pee Pee pulled the damn thing closer and snatched its plug from the wall. He had to get out of there.

Swinging his legs from the bed, he slowly inched his way to his feet. His muscles protested. They were stiff from weeks of disuse. He gritted his teeth. He would push through the pain. Grabbing the cane from beside the bed, he leaned heavily on it, testing his balance. The weight of his body felt foreign, a little uneven. The therapy had helped, but every step reminded him that he wasn't the man he used to be — well, not yet. His torso throbbed with every movement, and the memory of bullets was still fresh in his mind. The scar under his head dress tingled as if reminding him how close he'd come to never waking up at all.

He took slow, measured steps forward, feeling some strain on his abdomen. His breaths came short and shallow, each step forward a battle between his body's weakness and his will. However, Pee Pee wasn't about to let a few bullets stop him. He was getting out of here. No more waiting. No more hospital beds. No more pity. There was work to do and revenge to seek.

Stopping at the small table, Pee Pee picked up the receiver and dialed the only number he knew. The line would ring a few times before the person answered.

"Say…" he said into the phone. "I need a ride like yesterday. Look for me at the parking deck." He then hung the phone up.

Pee Pee glanced at the clock on the wall. He had close to twenty minutes before the first shift nurse came to check on him. That was all the time he had to slip out of the hospital before anyone noticed he was gone. He shifted his weight onto the cane, grimacing as the ache in his torso flared up. Every movement was a reminder of how messed up he was, but that didn't matter. He had to move.

Cautiously, he inched his way out of the room, keeping his head low while making his way down the corridor. The steady click of his cane against the tile floor seemed like it was echoing throughout the hallway, and each step felt like it would draw the wrong attention. Focusing on the task, he ignored the burn in his abdomen and the burning twinge in his scalp. He needed to get through the maze of corridors without being spotted.

Every nurse and doctor that passed by was a potential threat because they could stop him at any moment and ask where he was going. *Then what?* He kept close to the wall, avoiding all eye contact.

By the time he reached the stairwell, his breath was coming in short gasps, and a thin layer of sweat began to coat his face. The elevator wasn't an option — too risky, too exposed. Gripping the cane tighter, he pushed open the stairwell door and began his slow descent down the stairs. Each step was a test of his very own endurance.

He had to pause halfway and lean against the cold railing. His head began to spin for a moment. *Get it together*, he thought. Hot was probably outside by now, so he saw this as his only shot to make it out. Pee Pee wiped the sweat from his forehead and began moving again. The ticking of the clock in his mind grew louder with each minute that passed. He pushed the exit door open.

Glancing around the garage, Pee Pee looked for any signs of security or staff. The fluorescent lights overhead cast a glow in the middle of the rows of cars. The dark areas were perfect for him to limp in. He wiped the sweat from his brow with the back of his hand, feeling a sting of exhaustion creep its way through his body. He knew Hot had to be waiting nearby, but there was no room for mistakes or tiredness.

Shuffling toward the far end of the garage, he tapped the cane against the concrete floor with each step. Every sound echoed louder in his ears, but he couldn't afford to stop now. He reached the last row of cars where he spotted Hot's whip — an old, black sedan — with the engine idling. Relief poured over him.

With one last surge of energy, Pee Pee limped for the car, the cool air hitting his face as he stepped out of the shadows of the garage. The passenger door swung open. Hot leaned out, scanning him up and down. "You good, fam?"

"Yeah," Pee Pee muttered, sliding into the seat, wincing from the pain in his side. "Just drive."

———

AN HOUR LATER, Pee Pee stood shirtless in the bathroom of Hot's place, staring in the mirror at his beaten reflection. He studied the etched scars of his torso. The lines were jagged, angry reminders of how close death had come to claiming him. Two long scars marked his chest where the bullets had torn through with another scar running along his side, just under his ribs. He traced the rough edges with his fingertips, his face tightening as the memories surged back. Each scar was a symbol of pain, survival, and the person he'd lost.

He let out a slow breath and pulled the shirt on. There wasn't time to dwell on the pain. He'd survived for a reason. Pee Pee clenched his fists, feeling that fire ignite in his chest — burning hotter than the pain. They were going to pay. Every last one of them.

He turned away from the mirror, grabbing his cane. There was no more time to waste.

"You good?" questioned Hot who'd been spinning a pistol on the kitchen table the entire time Pee Pee was in the bathroom. He hated that his partner had gotten fucked over by some niggas. Though he was more than glad he'd survived it.

Pee Pee nodded, meeting Hot's inquiring gaze. "Shid, ain got no choice but to be good."

Hot stopped the pistol mid-spin and leaned back in the chair. "So, who the fuck did this shit to you? Since you didn't answer the question in the car." His eyes became intense as the question lingered in the air a few seconds. Hot couldn't understand why Pee Pee had avoided the question, along with any form of communication, in the car. He'd seen a few niggas recover from being shot before, so he knew that shock and confusion could mess with a man's mind. But Pee Pee was different. He'd been silently off, like something deeper was eating at him.

"Nigga, there's a time for that. Right now, I need to know who running the show?" Pee Pee asked, limping his way to the counter for the pain pills he had Hot grab out of a Walgreens they were passing.

Hot looked at him closely a moment. "Shawty, some niggas killed Bla…"

"Nigga, I know that," Pee Pee snapped after chewing down four pills. "Who the fuck running shit?"

Hot placed his elbows on the table and rubbed his chin. "Shid, Tip…"

"Tip?" Pee Pee knew the name and story all too well. Tip was a brown skin, medium built, chain gang nigga from Savannah, Georgia. He came to the city looking for a quick come-up to take home and ended up catching a ten year stretch in prison — all thanks to a dude's statement. Right after completing his sentence, he came back to Atlanta with revenge set in his heart. It would take him no more than two weeks to find who he was looking for, a guy by the name of Geo who was a part of Black Hand. This revelation threw a big curve in Tip's plan.

But he wouldn't be easily deterred. He would wait another two weeks before being presented with an opportunity. His ear had been to the streets. He'd heard so many tales about Black and the Hand that he decided to play it smart. First, he needed to put a face on the man in charge. Second, he needed to convince the guy that one of his soldiers was a rat. After weeks of watching, he decided to take a chance. Members of *the Hand* were throwing a *get together* for the entire hood when he made his move.

Walking along the packed street, Tip weaved between the crowd until his feet touched the yard. He noticed how little the nigga had changed. Geo was a few feet away, leaning on the porch rail, laughing and enjoying life in the presence of two bad bitches. Tip smirked, taking a glance around his surroundings. He needed to find another face if he wanted to leave with his life after doing what he came to do. Darting his eyes in the direction of his target every couple of seconds, he merged into the background of the crowd where he patiently waited. A little over an hour would pass before the stage was set for his performance.

The sun was setting when Black showed up with a ten-man entourage who escorted him toward the house. And Geo had drunk enough to piss out a river. Stumbling off from a female, Geo made his way around the side of the house. Tip followed at a distance to make sure no one would ruin the surprise. He treaded nonchalantly, glancing over his shoulder here and there, until he found the man of the hour. His pants were down, and he was caught.

Tip would force Geo at gunpoint to the front of the house with his pants at his ankles. This was about to be the moment of truth for both of them. A few onlookers would laugh at the sight of the half-nude man before they realized that the person a step behind him had a gun glued to the back of his head. Some individuals would disperse, while others trained their weapons on the armed imposter. Abruptly, the party stopped, bringing forth every nigga concerned in the matter — which was every member of the Hand present.

Never in his life had so many guns been aimed at him. But he was too far over the line to think about crossing back. Using his co-defendant as a shield, Tip maneuvered Geo toward whoever got close. The shouts and screams carried on for a minute and some before the man himself stepped out, silencing everyone. Tip had to admit that he was astounded by the man's aura of authority. It alone had caused every mouth to shut-the-fuck-up. Without hesitation, Tip reached under his shirt, bringing out a manila envelope. Fearlessly, Black stepped toward them until he was within arm's reach. The rest was history.

Black would listen and read the contents of the envelope carefully. Geo would be dead within minutes — with his pants down. And Tip? He would rise quickly, becoming a member of the Hand, reaching the status of lieutenant in just a few months — due to his viciousness and unyielding self-reliance for survival. These two things had made him, and Pee Pee was thinking of how those two things were about to break him.

"Yeah, nigga, the Tip you thinking bout. When that shit went down with Black, you know niggas started saying all types of shit and reaching for whatever they could grab. You was out the picture, so dude felt he had to step up to keep shit from falling apart…"

"How convenient for him and how stupid of y'all. A nigga who ain't been a part of this family a full year steps up and into the shoes that he's been trying to fill ever since he pulled that lil stunt at the spot. The fuck wrong with y'all?"

"Nigga, ain't no *y'all*. Them niggas," Hot barked, boring into the inquisitive face. Since Pee Pee's first call, Hot dreaded the moment when he'd have to say what had to be said. A lot had changed in the little time he'd been gone.

"What you saying?" Pee Pee leaned against the counter, studying the other person in life he'd die for. He placed one hand on top of the other, keeping the cane in place.

Hot returned Pee Pee's stare. There was no need to beat around the bush. "Shawty, ain part of that shit no more."

"*That shit…*" Pee Pee mocked, offering a faint chuckle. Turning, he grabbed the pill bottle again, dumping two more into his palm. He needed to douse the fire which Hot's words had ignited again. "Maybe you somehow forgot that *that shit* is why you have this *shit!*" With that, Pee Pee swept the cane around, indicating the entire condo.

"No, nigga, the blood *we* lost and the work *we* put in is why I got *this*. Just a few weeks ago, you was dead as Black is, and none of them niggas gave two fucks about what had happened to Pee Pee. But I did — every fucking day I did. So how the fuck would I look staying down wit some niggas that don't give a fuck about my nigga?" Hot rubbed his hands together, watching his fragile friend closely. "Pee, we don't need them nigg…"

"How the fuck you know what I need?" Pee Pee snarled, catching Hot off guard with the remark. "And it ain't about staying down wit niggas. It's about keeping what the fuck belongs to us. Nigga, how long we been a part of the Hand? How many days of work we done put in to keep this muthafucka up? Shawty, I understand the love, but I'm one nigga. Black was the forerunner, yet still he was one nigga. So, how the hell did the fates of two people turn over a whole damn kingdom?"

Hot arched an eyebrow, confused. Then, he shook his head in disbelief. The words were hitting him differently. "Bra, what damn kingdom? The hell is you talking bout? Nigga, that shit wasn't no kingdom. It was just a clique of us doing what we had to do to survive. You talking like we was on some royalty shit or some'n." Hot released a light chuckle. "Ain't nobody out here wearing no crowns, Pee."

Pee Pee's jaw clenched. He wanted badly to correct this nigga, but he didn't have the time to give a lesson right now. There were other things on his mind. "Hot, I'm going back to the Hand, and I'm taking back everything. You either gone be with me or not."

Hot leaned back in his chair, shaking his head a bit. "Bra, I get it. You feel like you owe it to Black, like you got to make shit right. But what's to make right? The Hand has changed. It's nothing like it was. And even then, it wasn't a kingdom…" Hot's words trailed off. He stared at the person who'd been with him through it all. A deep breath escaped his nostrils before he continued. "Look, Pee, you know how this nigga, Tip, get down. It's gonna be a lot of bloodshed if you try this nigga. Niggas are riding his wave high and hard and are ready to die in his cause. These niggas are not who they were when Black was in the picture. They changed along with the situation. But if it's what you wanna do, then I'm with you, my nigga. I only got one condition you need to meet."

An eyebrow rose as he stared at his friend curiously. Then, he gave a nod for him to go on.

"Firstly…"

"Nigga, you said *only one*," Pee Pee said, quickly reminding him.

"Man, I know what the fuck I said." Hot smiled. "But on some real shit, you got to get yourself together…" His retinas landed on the walking stick. "Ain't no way in hell I'ma be out waging a damn war wit a barely walking, crippled ass nigga." That brought a laugh from both of them.

"Nigga, I'm far from crippled. Just got a few kinks to straighten out…"

"A few kinks? Nigga, please!" Hot shook his head amusingly. "You looked like a nigga granddaddy making a slow ass escape from a nursing home. Ya ass was in turtle speed the entire way to the car…"

"Man, fuck you." Pee Pee laughed. But Hot was right. He wasn't in any type of condition to be going to war with someone of Tip's caliber. Tip — alone — was a force to be reckoned with. The man was relentless and a problem Pee Pee hadn't fully figured out how to deal with yet. And adding artillery and an army of niggas to the equation placed him above any obstacle Pee Pee had ever thought about trying to climb.

He exhaled slowly. The weight of the situation was beginning to press down on his mental. Bullets had torn into his body. His scars were still fresh, and his strength wasn't exactly there. Going up against Tip and the Hand wouldn't be just a challenge. It would be a death sentence unless he played it smart.

Tapping the walking cane on the kitchen's floor, Pee Pee's mind began working through the angles. Physically, he wasn't ready, but he would be. If there was one thing Pee Pee learned from Black, it was how to survive. And right now, survival meant stepping back to find the right edge he'd need in taking Tip down.

Nine Months Later

"You got the niggas, Live and Bo, holding down this lil spot. This where Tip usually be at," Hot said to Pee Pee as the rain slapped against the windshield. The sky above was dark, storming clouds over Lithonia. The two sat in the car, staring through the rain-soaked window at one of Tip's spots which sat across the street from them. The dim lights on the inside flickered through the downpour, letting them know that someone was inside the house. The distant rumbling of thunder matched the upsetting rumble of Pee Pee's gut.

For months, he'd been preparing himself for this very moment. Nine months of pushing through the pain, forcing his body back into shape. Every night, every scar burned from thoughts of that dreadful night he'd been left under that pole.

Now, he'd finally rebuilt himself, physically and mentally, brick by brick, refueling the burning urge for revenge. He'd pay back all of those niggas who had thought Pee Pee was done, especially the ones who'd left him for dead. They would all see that he wasn't just coming back but that he was coming for everything. And Tip was the first step. He had watched, had planned, and now had reached the moment to set it all in motion.

Rain slid down the passenger's window in heavy droplets. Pee Pee's focus remained steady. They didn't see the metallic black Corvette Z06 which Hot said he drove. Tip's absence put a slight dent in his plans but not enough where they'd have to put it off. He had something else in mind.

"So, what we doing?" Hot asked, wiping fog from his side of the window.

Pee Pee knew both Live and Bo — two low level niggas who'd joined the Hand in the last two years like Tip had. They had been recruited as shooters, so them holding down any type of spot was comical and slightly dangerous for what he was thinking.

"Shid, their actions gonna determine that once they see I'm back. They either get wit it or get shitted on." Pee Pee snatched the slide backwards on the SIG Sauer and pulled the hoodie over the skull cap he had on his head. The two stepped out into the rain, water splashing under their feet as they lightly sprinted across the street, heading straight for the porch of their destination. The rain couldn't wash away the tension — nor the intentions.

The rain poured off the edges of the porch roof as Pee Pee and Hot reached the steps. Water dripped from their soaked hoodies as they knocked on the burglar bar door. A small, static-filled crackle came from the speaker mounted above the doorbell.

"Who the fuck is y'all?" a voice rasped through the speaker, sounding suspicious and agitated.

Pee Pee leaned closer to the door, wiping rain off his face with the back of his hand. "Nigga, it's Pee Pee."

There was a too long pause before a low grunt came from the other end. "Turn to the camera," the voice commanded with a hint of impatience.

Pee Pee glanced at Hot, both of them realizing they'd forgotten about the small security camera tucked away in the corner with its lens blinking. They turned, facing the camera, pulling both their hoodies down. They stood still as the red light continued to blink. The rain continued to beat down around them, but it felt like the entire world had paused in that moment. After a few tense seconds, there was another crackle from the speaker.

"Aight," Bo's voice finally said, followed by the faint sound of locks turning on the other side of the door. Pee Pee took a deep breath, his jaw tightening. It was time to remind niggas.

The door cracked open, and Bo's pudgy ass stood in the doorway with a grin that didn't quite match his eyes. His skin was still dark as the night, and the surprise was poorly hidden. His hand lingered on the edge of the door as if he was deciding whether to open it wider or slam it in their faces.

"Boy, look who it is. Pee Pee and muthafucking Hot," Bo said, voice anything but genuine. He looked Pee Pee up and down. Bo's eyes narrowed despite the smile still etched on his face. "Boy, ain expect to see you again, my nigga. The fuck happened?"

"Had a lil accident, but I'm good," Pee Pee said, stepping inside with Hot following suit. He could feel the unspoken tension between them, yet he nodded, keeping his face neutral. Pee Pee understood the assignment. This wasn't a reunion but a test.

"A lil accident?" Pee Pee heard the familiar voice say from somewhere to the left of him. Pee-Pee's eyes shifted, catching the figure just outside of his line of sight. It was Live, standing with his arms crossed. The man hadn't changed a bit — stocky build, thick neck, the same piercing gaze that always made you think twice before speaking.

Live took a step forward, his eyes narrowing as he looked Pee Pee up and down, measuring him. "Shid, niggas made it seem like you got took out the day before that shit went down with Black." Live placed his eyes on Hot. "I know Hot already gave you the rundown on how that played out?"

Pee Pee rubbed his chin. "Yeah — that's exactly why I need to talk to Tip."

Live stared at him a moment, undecided on whether or not he should let this nigga holla at Tip. He knew how things worked around there. And Pee Pee showing up wasn't part of that operation. Tip had built something solid since Black went down, and if Pee Pee thought he was about to fuck up that balance, he thought wrong. Live studied him another moment then scratched the back of his head. "Aight, I'ma hit the nigga," he said, moving for his phone.

"Look at this nigga. Ain't been back from the dead a full thirty minutes and already making requests," Bo said sarcastically, letting the smirk return to his face.

Pee Pee didn't react to the remark. He kept his eyes locked on Live as he placed the phone next to his ear. His mind raced, thinking about how Tip would respond after hearing he was back in the picture. Pee Pee knew better than to expect anything close to a warm reception. Too much had changed since he disappeared. Tip had taken over after Black was killed, filling the power vacuum like it was made for him. And with Pee Pee presumed dead, Tip had solidified his grip on the Hand, expanding his influence and building a foundation he wasn't likely to give up without some death. Plus, Pee Pee's sudden return wasn't just an unexpected twist. It was a threat. Tip would most likely try to welcome him back as an ally, just to keep watch of him. If anyone could remove him, it was Pee Pee.

Live's expression was unreadable as he spoke into the phone. "Yo, Tip… Yeah, you ain't gonna believe this. How bout this nigga, Pee Pee, done returned?" There was a pause as Live listened to the response on the other end. Pee Pee tried to read his body language, but Live stayed stone faced, keeping whatever reaction Tip was having to himself.

A moment passed, and the silence between them was thick and heavy. Then, Live abruptly held the phone out toward Pee Pee. "He wants to talk to you."

Pee Pee took the phone, already knowing that whatever came next was going to set the tone for everything that followed. He lifted it to his ear, catching the tension in Tip's voice before he even spoke.

"Pee Pee," Tip said slowly, the edge unmistakable. "What's good with you, dirty? Where the fuck you been?"

Live shot Bo a side glance which Pee Pee immediately caught. The corner of his mouth inched upward. "Out of commission," Pee Pee let out, keeping his voice cool and smooth. "You kn…"

"He had a lil accident!" Bo said, cutting in loudly.

Pee Pee faced him, irritated. "Yeah, a lil accident that took me a minute to get back on my feet from. But I'm here now." He let his last words hang in the air a few moments. Bo had leaned against the wall indifferently, and Pee Pee noticed.

"Is that right?" Tip finally replied. Pee Pee could tell by the sound of his voice that Tip wasn't interested in the mishap. It was filled with suspicion. "Okay, you back, dirty, so what's good?"

"You tell me since you the one running the show now."

"And gone continue running it," Tip stated matter-of-factly. "Pee, it's been what, ten months, eleven, since niggas heard anything from you? It's funny how you just suddenly went MIA right before the shit jumped off wit Black. Now here you are… back? What should I make of this?"

Pee Pee could easily see where this was going. So, why not beat him there by putting it all on the table? "Nigga, make what the fuck you feel outta it, but I got holes in me to prove where the fuck I been. That's some shit we'll get to later. Right now though, you in the wrong seat, my boy. Black s…" Tip cut him off.

"Pee, pump ya brakes, dirty. I know you was Black right hand and all, but you wasn't here when he needed you. And you damn sure wasn't here when some of these greedy ass niggas were bout to cause this shit to crumble…"

"Nigg…" Pee Pee began, but Tip wasn't finished.

"Dirty, hol on… When you went ghost, nigga, I stood on business and held this shit together — not just for me but, nigga, for all of *us* — and Black. Pee, believe me when I tell you that I had more than enough reason to take what the fuck I could — which would of been most of it — and leave the Hand to crash. But I didn't, even after a few niggas took aim at my head. Nah, I weathered the storm and dealt with those who didn't give a fuck about keeping Black's legacy alive. Hell, I even made things a lil better within these last few months — in case you haven't asked niggas."

Pee Pee nodded his head as if he cared about what Tip was saying. His ears were deaf and insensitive to anything that wasn't in line with his predetermined goals. Pivoting, his eyes found Bo was still leaning against the wall. He smirked when Live began to move toward the kitchen. He already knew that Hot was following every bit of Live's body, but Live wasn't the one Pee Pee was really concerned about. "Shid, that's what's up. And a nigga preciate you holding shit dow…"

Tip still wasn't done. "But like you said, Pee, you back. And I can respect that because I respect you. But on some real nigga shit, I ain't moving out of this muthafucking seat. So, how bout this? Let's get together and first clear up a few things for everybody who wants to know the reason behind the Houdini shit. Then, *we* let the Hand figure out exactly where you're going to fit in at. Smooth?"

His jawbone clenched. "Okay, cool. When and where we meeting at? We can do this today." Pee Pee scratched the back of his neck with his index finger, signaling Hot.

"Say, Live, what y'all niggas got to drink on?" Hot said, moving toward him. That caused Bo to straighten his posture. He eyed Hot down suspiciously.

"Cool, my brother," Tip said. "Put Live back on. He'll bring you to me."

"I'ma put you on speaker…"

Tip let out a chuckle. "Man, nigga, ain't nobody on no slick shit, Pee. You fam, bro."

"Probably, but Ion think Bo seeing it that way."

"Seeing what?" Bo questioned. He took his eyes off Hot as he stepped closer to Pee Pee.

Pee Pee immediately noticed how Bo's hand had slid around his side. He hit the speaker icon. "Tip say he want y'all to take me to 'em." Pee Pee extended the phone toward Bo, who quickly snatched it from his hand.

"Bra-bra…" was all Bo would get out. Within an instant, Pee Pee whipped out the Sauer, shooting Bo right in the stomach. "Fuc…" Bo stumbled backwards, dropping the phone. Pee Pee would hear only a small portion of the rumble in the kitchen before he shot Bo twice in the face. Quickly, he turned and saw Hot sling Live into the refrigerator door by his collar as he shoved the end of the barrel into his cheek.

"Bo… Bo, what the fuck going on? Pee…" Pee Pee could hear Tip ranting from the phone. He picked it up and smiled.

"Tip, slow down…"

"Nigga, what the fuck you done did?" Tip yelled through the speaker.

"I just killed Bo…"

"Pee, what the fuc…"

"Aye, shut the fuck up and listen. Nigga, I'm not settling for anything less than Black's throne, ight? And I'ma have it one way or another. So, either you step the fuck down and let all them other disloyal muthafuckas know that you handing it to its rightful owner, or

I kill every nigga that thinks otherwise." Pee Pee pointed with the gun, signaling for Hot to move Live to the couch.

A moment of intense silence passed, then he heard Tip clear his throat. "Pee, you sure you wanna play it like this? I mean, dirty, let's be for real. Damn near every nigga in the Hand think you had something to do with Black getting killed. Then you come back, killing other members because you want to fill Black's shoes. Pee, who in the hell you think is gonna side with you against me at this point?" Tip let out a halfhearted chuckle.

"I only killed one. Live is still living. Wanna talk to him?" Pee Pee held out the phone, offering Live a smile.

"Live?" Tip called out.

"Yeah…" The word sounded awkward coming out of his mouth because Hot kept the pistol launched under his cheekbone.

"Dirty… brother, you know it's all love at the end of the day between us. But it ain't nothing I can say or do to save you, so make peace with God, my nigga." The phone's sudden quietness made Pee Pee turn the screen back to him. Tip had hung up.

Pee Pee wanted to laugh. "Damn, it's crazy that the nigga you pledged loyalty to would just up and leave you hanging between life and death."

"Bee Bee, rra…" The barrel in his jaw was making his words hard to understand.

"Hot, let up…" Pee Pee wanted to hear what the man had to say. Hopefully, it was something he could use in the war against Tip and his followers.

"Pee Pee, bra, please don't do thi…"

"Live…" Pee Pee began, sliding the coffee table back to take a seat. "I'ma make this simple as possible. Do you want to see another day?"

"Man, fuck that. This nigga ain't seeing shit," Hot said, placing the sight of the gun on his temple. Letting a nigga live was not a part of the original plan.

Pee Pee stood and stepped over the small space between them.

Making eye contact, Pee Pee placed a hand on the barrel of Hot's gun and slowly forced it away from Live's head.

"Pee, what the fuck, man? Ain't no way we gon leave this nigga alive. Nigga, he done seen both our faces an…"

"Nigga, is you scared?" Pee Pee asked, cutting him off. "Or have you forgotten the oath you took too?"

"Oath? Pee, we don't have tim…"

"Don't have time for what?" Pee Pee's voice was sharp and unwavering. "To remember the vows you both pledged to Black Hand? Have you niggas forgotten that it was the oath that built our empire? We all promised to be our brother's keeper, and now don't nobody fucking remember because Black dead?"

The room became still a moment while Pee Pee's words hung in the air like small fragments of existence. He could now grasp what Tip had said. Black was out of the picture, and niggas saw no need in holding on to the values Black had planted within them. His absence alone had obviously tossed every rule the Hand was founded on to the side. This reminded him why he was the one chosen to put every piece of the Hand back as it should be. And he would.

"Those vows didn't expire when Black died. You swore your lives to them, the same as I did." Pee Pee switched his eyes between both of them until they settled on Hot. Hot, countless of times, had stood by him and the decisions he'd made. And for the first time, he found himself questioning where Hot's feet were planted. "Hot, you been my nigga forever, but my loyalty is wit the Hand. So, it's either you wit me on this or not. Make your choice now."

Hot stared at the only real friend he had in the world. He hated the fact that he was forcing him to choose between him and the thing he never wanted to be a part of in the first place. Pee Pee had made the choice to join, and Hot followed because he was a follower. Had always been if he wanted to be honest about it. Hot didn't possess the drive and ambition of a leader. Those were always Pee Pee's traits, which was why he followed him.

Right now though, he wasn't sure if continuing to do so was in his best interest. Black had been killed and Pee Pee hospitalized by people who could have easily been members of the Hand — which at times he thought was the case. Pee Pee wasn't there to witness it unfold from the time of Black's death to the bloody struggles for Black's power. Yet he'd seen it all and had decided to step away before he ended up with his head on the chopping block. Now here was the only nigga he was loyal to asking for him to aid in the losing battle for that very same power.

Hot shook his head because he couldn't understand it, and as well, he couldn't just let Pee Pee fight alone. He knew that his absence would definitely minimize Pee Pee's chances of taking down Tip — if he actually had any.

"Pee, just know if I die, my blood will be on your hands. And only yours," Hot told him, shaking the pistol at him.

A smirk appeared on Pee Pee's face. He already knew Hot wasn't going to be the one to let him down. Never had been. "Nigga, it's not only gonna be your blood." Pee Pee set his retinas on their hostage. "Live, I remember when you was nothing. A nobody. A simple ass nigga without a pot to piss in. Then you was embraced by Black Hand, and all that shit changed immediately. –Nigga, how many days since then have you been a nobody with nothing?"

"None, Pee," Live said, staring daggers into Pee Pee.

"None. So why the fuck would you step off that solid platform Black had situated for your feet?"

"I didn't, nigga. I'm still part of the Hand."

"No the fuck you not," Pee Pee snapped. "You part of the shit Tip molded it into. That ain't the Hand and will never be long as that country ass nigga calling shots when you — like every other nigga — know who the fuck pose to be in that seat. There was a set list that Black put in place for leadership when shit happened, and Tip was nowhere on it. Did you know the list?"

Live nodded his head because every person within the Hand had to memorize it.

"Okay, roll call, nigga." Pee Pee folded his arms across his chest, waiting patiently.

"Black, you, Slug, and Face…"

"Good. Black died, I was out of the picture, so what the fuck happened to Slug and Face?" Hot had already told Pee Pee what happened to the two, but he wanted to see if Live was going to be a hundred with him. This was going to be a major factor in deciding his fate.

"Man, when niggas got wind of Black's death, a few niggas saw an opportunity and went for it. They killed Slug and Face the…"

"On whose orders?" Pee Pee asked.

"Chief. He sent his lil squad to shoot both of them down…"

"Which everybody, even his lil shooters, should of known was in violation, right?"

Live nodded then dropped his head.

"So, who took the initiative to right the wrong? I'm curious." Pee Pee also had knowledge of this, again thanks to Hot.

"Tip. Bra was mad about what them niggas had done. He grabbed a few niggas that didn't like the shit either and went to war with Chief and his lil clan…"

Pee Pee felt the urge to cut him off. "Well, I would say he went to war with Chief specifically because wasn't Chief the only one to die on *that* side of the fence?"

Again, Live nodded, agreeing.

"And I'm guessing you joined Tip cause his move seemed to be righteous?"

"Nigga, yeah." Live said it like he didn't regret a minute of it.

Pee Pee couldn't believe how naïve some of these dudes were. When Hot had relayed the story to him, it didn't take long for him to see the bigger picture. The names alone had carved out the outline perfectly. "Now tell me this. Why would Tip *righteously* go after and kill a nigga who followed him more than his own back pockets? Stupid ass nigga, Chief was Tip's crony, and he would of never made anything close to a move like that unless it was greenlighted by Tip first."

Live raised a curious eyebrow. It was his first time hearing this, and the fact that it was falling from Pee Pee's mouth made it believable. There had only been one nigga above Pee Pee on the letter of rank, so if anybody was in the know, it would be him.

"Yeah, he fooled all you niggas. Anyway, ain gonna kill you, but I'ma offer you two choices, one being you joining and helping me put the Hand back where it supposed to be. And the other is you leaving this city for good because once I leave here and you're still alive, how do you think Tip is going to feel about it?" Pee Pee sat down next to Live on the couch. "I really don't think he'll be as gracious as I am. And since we're running low on time, I need you to quickly tell us where everything is at, then you can make your choice. Cool?"

Looking at Pee Pee then Hot, Live began nodding again, silently praying that the second choice was actually possible.

———

Now, what's taking them so long? thought the man. His grip tightened around the binoculars he'd had glued to his face ever since the two unknowns had stepped onto the porch. The rain beat down heavily, distorting his view and forcing him to adjust his position. For more than six weeks, him and his small team had been taking turns keeping this property under close surveillance. Over the course of the last few weeks, they had seen more than enough incriminating activity to meet the standards for a probable cause warrant. But luckily for the perpetrators, no part of their stake out had been authorized. Which meant making an arrest was the furthest thing from their minds.

"We got action," he said to his partner in the passenger seat. The agent watched as three figures emerged from the house, each carrying black duffle bags in both hands. Rolling down the driver's side window a bit to get a better look, he noticed the bulges at the bottom of the bags. From experience, this suggested that something of valuable weight was on the inside. This brought a smile to his face because not only did the occurrence present a possible payday, but it also presented a chance to finally show Eric Dunlap, a.k.a. Tip, why his arrogant ass should take advantage of a courteous gesture when offered.

Thunder cracked across the sky above as the bags were loaded into the trunk of the car they'd showed up in. "Where the plate numbers?"

the driver asked while watching the two individuals slip into the vehicle.

"Right here." The passenger waved the wet piece of paper with running ink in front of his face.

"Call Ronnie and tell him we need a unit to do a traffic stop and not any old unit. We need one of *his* units." The driver watched the prize vehicle pull away and create some distance between them before he turned over the ignition. It would have been a rookie move to do it any sooner. Slowly, he pulled into traffic as the voice of his passenger giving the description of their fleeing vehicle filled his ears.

———

"Pee, you outta fucking control," Hot said as they rode.

"Nigga, how?" Pee Pee returned. His eyes were locked on the contact list he was strolling through on Live's phone. He couldn't believe that Live had programed damn near every nigga's name from the Hand into this device. It was a gold mine of connections but as well a Fed case waiting to happen. How could Live be so reckless and unconcerned about walking around with an entire R.I.C.O. indictment in his pocket?

"How? Nigga, not only did you put Tip on point bout the move we making against him, but you let this nigga, Live, live after he watched you kill Bo. What the hell kind of sense was you trying to make?" Hot questioned incredulously.

Seeing enough of the contacts, Pee Pee lifted his eyes to the rain-soaked streets beyond the windshield. "Shawty, I wasn't trying to make sense…"

"Well, thank you for clearing that up cause the shit didn't make any sense!" Hot flicked on the defrost system. Their breath — mainly Hot's — were making it hard to see.

"It may not now, but eventually, it will. You just got to trust me," Pee Pee stated firmly. He didn't expect for Hot to see it from his point of view because Hot's vision was short sighted. He always focused on the here and now instead of the then and there. It was like his entire world had been placed into a tiny box which he didn't plan on escaping. How easily could his mindset be compared to a life in prison — something restrained and caged until the willpower to break free was finally found.

"I do trust you. I just don't agree with your logic on certain shit. You played the situation wrong with Live. I got to tell you that. We should of deaded that nigga along with Bo. He picked his side, ju…"

Pee Pee began to massage the bridge of his nose. He could feel a migraine slowly inching its way to the front of his brain. "Hot, have you ever read *The Art of War* by Sun Tzu? Or how bout *The Prince* by Niccolò Machiavelli?"

Hot gave Pee Pee a disgusted look. "Ni-nigga, hell nawl. I deal with reality. The shit that works out here in the real world."

"Stupid ass boy, books are reflections of reality and the real world, in case you didn't know. But them two books you need to read. Both books are based on military strategy and how to use the people you've conquered to tip the scales of war in your favor while expanding your power. See, we could of killed Live, but what would that have accomplished? Nothing. Would his death put us in a better position? Fuck no…"

"Shid, would his life?" Hot said, cutting him off.

"It could if used right. Think about it. We don't really know shit about Tip's set up, but Live could tell us. Just like he told us about the money that we didn't know nothing about…"

"Nigga, that was only because his life was on the line. Don't think that lil pep talk you gave him changed anything. I'm willing to bet that soon as we were out of Live's sight, he went and told Tip everything. Pee, these ain't the same niggas. Please get that through ya head."

Pee Pee stared at Hot a moment before speaking. "Shawty, why is you so pessimistic? That's the problem with Black people. They see nothing but the worst in their own kind."

"Man, ain trying to hear all that shit." Hot chuckled, waving him off.

"Well, you need to. How the hell…" Pee Pee's words trailed off once he noticed the police cruiser behind them. Even with the drops of rain scattered about the rearview mirror, he still couldn't mistake the car for anything else.

"How the hell what?" Hot asked.

"Twelve behind us," Pee Pee said, his voice low and steady though his muscles were tense. He kept his posture as still as possible, not wanting to draw any unnecessary attention. With guns in the car and a trunk full of money, getting pulled over wasn't just bad — it was a potential disaster waiting to happen.

"Damn," Hot huffed out the side of his mouth. They were on Panola Road, a four-lane street with a steady flow of traffic. Hot doubted his chances of outrunning the Dekalb County police in a chase and pulling off a successful getaway. Cars clogged the road ahead, and the ones in the left lane boxed him in. His only real option was to jump the curb, plow through a patch of thick bushes, and hope the car would glide across someone's lawn without getting stuck.

"Just chill, he probably ain't..." Pee Pee's words were cut short by the sudden, sharp chirp of the police siren. The sound sliced through the air, and his heart sank. "Fuck," he grumbled under his breath as blue lights flashed through the car, casting a blue glow over everything.

Hot's knuckles turned ashen as his grip tightened around the steering wheel, the tension radiating through his body. His anxiety was painfully obvious. "Pee, what we doing?" His voice wavered slightly, urgency creeping in. Hot needed Pee Pee's input before his nerves pushed him into making a rash decision.

Pee Pee ran a few scenarios through his head, none of which turned out good. Biting down on his bottom lip, he hated the fact that he had to take his chances under these circumstances. "Shid, pull over." The words sounded crazy to him and Hot.

"Pull over? Man..." Hot shook his head disappointedly. That was the last thing he wanted to hear.

"Nigga, it's a lose-lose all the way round the board. Let's just see what he talking bout." Doing as told, Hot crept the car into the parking lot of a closed church. It was like the rain started beating down harder on the hood of the car as soon as he slapped it in park and cut the car off.

Hot twisted his lips. "Shawty, Ion…"

"Shhh, positive energy," Pee Pee said, quickly cutting his words short before they jinxed them.

"Pos…" Hot bit his tongue. The frustration was evident as he lightly pounded a fist against his thigh. Not wanting to look at Pee Pee, Hot set his eyes on the rearview mirror and watched as the cop stepped out in his raincoat with the hood pulled over his head. Rain splashed over the inside of the door and Hot as he rolled the window. His heart began thumping to the rhythm of the downpour.

"How you doing, Officer?" Hot greeted the Caucasian male who had *racist pig* written all over his face. The man peered into the car first then asked for his license and registration.

"What's the problem, Officer?" Hot nervously shuffled through the papers of the glove compartment.

Pee Pee kept his gaze straight ahead, already aware that any look toward the policeman would arouse suspicion. Well, that was the excuse they always used to search a nigga's shit. His eyes flicked toward Hot's hand as he retrieved the documentation. When Pee Pee lifted his eyes again, something caught his attention in his peripheral vision. After a quick glance at the side mirror, he noticed that a black SUV had pulled in behind the police cruiser. *The fuck?* he thought as the passenger door swung open. A surge of uneasiness began to creep its way in.

Pee Pee's eyes narrowed, his heart pounding harder in his chest. The person stepped out of the SUV, dressed head to toe in black, a ski mask concealing his face. He looked more like he belonged to a special forces unit than someone conducting routine police business in the rain. Something felt off — way off. Pee Pee's pulse quickened, and just as he was processing the scene, he realized he hadn't noticed the second figure — another black-clad man — creeping up on Hot's side of the car.

"The hell?" Hot let out, looking at Pee Pee.

"And who do we have here?" the masked man asked, taking a good look at both of them. They could tell that he was smiling behind the mask. "How bout you step out for me, fellow?"

"What's going on?" Hot questioned, but the man was already pulling the door open.

"We about to find out. Place your hands on the roof for me. Do you have anything sharp on you that might harm me?" the masked man asked, kicking Hot's feet apart.

"No, man."

The other masked man had stopped at the trunk on Pee Pee's side; his presence was threatening. Pee Pee couldn't make out what he was saying to the uniformed officer, but he saw the cop nod, tossing Hot's credentials onto the roof carelessly before he left. Pee Pee knew Hot had to be furious. Not only were they stuck in a very bad situation, but now, Hot was being searched in the pouring rain, getting soaked to the bone.

"Can y'all tell us what's going on?" Pee Pee heard Hot say right before his door came open.

"Step out," the man flatly stated. Pee Pee did as instructed, glad that they'd stashed the guns under the seat. He looked over the man's attire and wondered why the insignia of who they were was missing.

The man's voice cut through the sound of the rain. Pee Pee's brow furrowed because somehow the voice seemed familiar, like he knew it but couldn't place it. The rain continued to pour as if the storm itself was closing in on them.

"Hands on the roof, Ricardo Diaz."

How they know my name? Pee Pee thought as he turned and met Hot's regretful gaze. He could hear the metallic cuffs click around Hot's wrists. What had he gotten them into?

"Anything on you?" he asked as the other guy lead Hot away.

"Nah," Pee Pee responded, bowing his head a bit to keep some of the rain out of his face.

"So, Mr. Diaz, what in the world have you been up to lately?" The man was talking like he knew him.

"Nothing that would invite a pat down from some fucking Navy Seals."

The guy laughed. "If we were Seals, your dick would have been in the mud by now. How bout you turn around for me."

Watching the other man return to the driver's side, Pee Pee pivoted around, meeting the icy blue eyes behind the mask. They too seemed familiar. "Are we under arrest, man?"

"No, not yet. But I'm glad to see that you finally came out the rabbit's hole and took some initiative."

"Ion know what you talking bout. I haven't took shit…"

"Sure, you did. I can see your confusion, so how bout I clear this up for you?" The man pulled the mask halfway up to reveal his face. Then, he smiled, exactly like he had at the hospital.

This muthafucka. Pee Pee thought he'd never see this particular person again yet here he stood, mere inches away from his face. "Agent Swift, *the asshole*, I should of known."

"Damn right you should have known — called — and maybe we wouldn't be out here right now enjoying this beautiful, wet day." Swift chuckled, pulling the mask back down over his face. "So, what's in the bags?"

Pee Pee glanced at the trunk with an arched eyebrow. He could hear the other guy rummaging through the interior of the car, which meant it was only a matter of time before he made his way to the rear. And him lying at this point would serve no purpose. "Financial backing."

"I figured as much." Getting the attention of his partner, Swift pointed at the trunk. Within a few seconds, the lock of the trunk clicked. "Uh, do I have to worry about you running?" Swift asked rhetorically.

"Do I need to run?" Pee Pee asked. His voice was low but tense, eyes switching between Swift and the trunk's lid lifting. His gaze then shifted to the SUV where they had placed Hot. The interior was shrouded in darkness, but he could make out the faint outline of Hot's figure through the rain-soaked windshield.

"Hopefully not." Swift leaned over, grabbing one of the duffle bags. Unzipping it, his retinas instantly locked on the bundles of money, which brought a loud whistle from his lips. "Damn. I see someone has placed themselves at the very top of Eric Dunlap's list of people to unalive. But who cares?" Swift said with a shrug of his shoulders. "How much is it?"

"Shid, Ion know because someone stopped us to have a wet ass chat in the rain," Pee Pee let out, beginning to feel the rain soak through the fabric of his clothing.

"Would you rather we have this chat back at the federal building? I can arrange it if that's what you want. But I seriously doubt that's the road you want to take." Swift's blue eyes bore into Pee Pee's as he patiently waited on a response.

After a few moments of silence, Swift said, "I didn't think so. Now give me a rough estimation."

Pee Pee's jaw clenched; his eyes swayed from Swift's unblinking stare to the ground. The threat broiled in the center of his chest, causing the anger to bubble under the surface of his skin. He hated the position they were in. It felt like he'd been cornered and pushed, yet he couldn't afford to let his emotions get the best of him. Definitely not right now. "It's a lil over a mill, possibly more."

"Jesus. Who would of thought Mr. Dunlap was stupid enough to leave that much money in such an unsecured place?" Swift said to his comrade, tapping his finger on the trunk's lid. The sound of thunder emitted from the clouds above, and Swift set his sight back on the person who was about to help him fix all his problems.

"Mr. Diaz, we have a lot of catching up to do. So, until then, three of these duffels are leaving with me," Swift added, signaling for his partner to start loading the bags into the SUV.

Moving quickly, the man lifted the bags from the trunk and hauled them to the SUV while Swift kept his gaze locked on Pee Pee. When the last bag was secured, Swift waved a hand toward his partner. "Let him out," he ordered, jerking his chin toward Hot, who was still sitting in the back of the SUV, frustrated.

The SUV door opened, and Hot stumbled out, glaring at the situation but staying quiet as the cuffs were taken off. Pee Pee could see that he was beyond nervous and mad, but there was no room for words right now.

Swift gave Pee Pee one last glance. "Once you get in touch, I'll let you know what the next phase is." With that, Swift turned, getting into the SUV. The vehicle rumbled to life and pulled away. Pee Pee continued to stand in the rain as Hot snatched the driver's door open and hopped in. He then did the same.

"Pee, what the fuck going on? And who was them muthafuckas?" Hot angrily questioned.

Pee Pee pulled the skull cap from his head and slung it out the window, then he wiped some of the rain from his face. "The fucking D.E.A. They was watching Tip's spot and seen us come out with the bags."

"So, you telling me you'n know that cracker who you was just talking to, and he don't know you?" Hot eyed him suspiciously.

"Nigga, hell nah," Pee Pee responded defensively. There was no way in hell he was about to tell him how he knew Swift. He'd have to kill Hot — or be killed.

"So, what the fuck was all that talking bout?"

"Nothing really. Him and his mans was just some more crooked ass cops on the prowl for a come up and caught us at the right time. The muthafucka started asking bout Tip and talking bout locking us up, so I told him that it was money in the trunk to get us out the jam. What? You had a better idea sitting in the backseat of that truck wit some fucking cuffs on?"

Hot stared at him another moment then turned the ignition switch. He felt that something wasn't right about the occurrence and that there was more than what Pee Pee was saying. But he'd hold his tongue. Whatever was in the dark always came to the light, he knew. "Aight, say less. I'ma take ya word for it, my nigga."

"Hot, my word is bond. You already know that though. Them crackers was laying and got a come up. I'm just glad they didn't take everything. We would have been back at square one. Shit would've been all bad then." Pee Pee looked out the window as they pulled out of the parking lot. The money Swift had taken wouldn't be missed. But nothing he'd put work in for was free. Swift had created a debt, and Pee Pee would figure out exactly how he'd make good on it.

The Meeting

"Let's not forget the people who took it and all the people who are desperately trying to get their hands on them." Pee Pee smiled, leaning back against the cushion of the chair. By the man's expression, he knew he had him exactly where they wanted him.

Asher stared at him a few seconds, searching his body language for any signs of deception. There were none. "And in return for this information, you want *in*?"

"Yes, but not *in* what you're thinking. It would be stupid as fuck for me to suggest your family's organization. I'm not Italian, so it a never happen. But when I say *in*, I'm meaning in the fucking enterprise of this great city. You see, I know how things work around here. The real power is in alliances — who controls what streets and businesses. And I want to be a part of that. Fuck the neighborhood hustling shit. I need to get into something bigger, like something that makes this whole city tick."

Pee Pee rested his interlocked fingers on his abdomen, letting his words settle. He could see the wheels turning in the other man's head. This wasn't about fitting into a box or an organization. This was about carving out his own space in the power structure. He just needed him to understand that it wasn't about what family you were born to. It was about what you could build.

Asher rubbed the barrel of the gun against his kneecap. Though it wasn't out of nervousness but was out of pure amusement. A small smirk appeared on his face. "You speak like you have it all figured out. But I doubt you do. This *enterprise* you talk about isn't just for anyone, you know? I've seen countless of men come and go because they — like you — thought that they actually possessed what it took to exceed on this level of the game.

"Some had the balls, others the brains… but the ones that mastered it? Well, they had something more. Something that would get any man through any situation. And that something was ambition."

Unblinking, Pee Pee met Asher's cold stare with his own. "That's *something* I have more than enough of."

Standing, Asher slid the gun into his waistband. "Maybe. But like everything else, ambition has a cost. You sure you would be able to make that payment?"

Pee Pee didn't flinch. "I'll die trying."

"Defiant. I like that." Asher slid two fingers around the edge of the mahogany desk as he walked back to his seat. "I'm going to run your name by a few people. If you turn out to be a decent person, I'll be in touch. And if not, I won't. It's pretty simple. Give your number to Aldo on your way out," Asher said, slouching back in his comfortable chair.

"Cool." Pee Pee stood, extending his hand for a handshake.

Asher's eyes went from his visitor's face to the extended limb and back to his face. He forced his lips into a broad smile. "I don't shake hands unless the business is complete, and our business is very far from that. Have a nice day."

Pee Pee gave him a mischievous smirk then turned, heading for the door. His hand was reaching for the knob when Asher asked, "By the way, what's your real name, and what do people call you?"

"Ricardo Diaz… But I'm Freshman Black, or you can just call me Black," Pee Pee told him then pulled the door open.

After giving the henchmen his contact information, Freshman Black exited the building. Soon as he got back in the rental he'd been driving for the past few days, he quickly retrieved his cell phone. Strolling through his call log, he found the unsaved number and rubbed his thumb over the call icon.

It took three rings for the man to answer. "How may I help?"

"I just left the manager at the grocery store. He said after they conduct a background check, he'll let me know if I'd be hired or not. But if you want my opinion, I'd say I got the job," Freshman Black said gladly.

"That is good news — very good news — which means that we can now set up the decorations for the surprise party you had in mind."

"I'm ready. And I came up with the best way you can assist me since it requires a certain can of expertise." Freshman Black thought that Agent Swift was about to be the perfect remedy to halt the contagious disease of Tip. A smile came to his face. He was about to become a king.

Did you enjoy the read?
Let us know how much by leaving us a review on Amazon and
Goodreads.

OTHER BOOKS BY

Urban Aint Dead

Tales 4rm Da Dale

The Hottest Summer Ever

Hittin' Licks For The Holidays: Atlanta

Wet Dreams On Lockdown: The Nurse

How To Publish A Book From Prison

By **Elijah R. Freeman**

Despite The Odds

By **Juhnell Morgan**

Good Girls Gone Rogue

Good Girls Gone Rogue 2

By **Manny Black**

Hittaz

Hittaz 2

Hittaz 3

Hittaz 4

Hittaz 5

Coldhearted

Coldhearted 2

Coldhearted 3

By **Lou Garden Price, Sr.**

Charge It To The Game

Charge It To The Game 2

A Summer To Remember With My Hitta

Snatched Up By A Hitta

Santa Sent Me A Real One For Christmas

Wet Dreams On Lockdown: The Unit Manager

Thug Me The Right Way 2

Thug Me The Right Way 3

Seizing A Gangsta's Heart For The Summer

Yours For The Taking

Wrapped Up In A Hitta's Love For Christmas

By **Nai**

A Set Up For Revenge

A Set Up For Revenge 2

Wet Dreams On Lockdown: The Librarian

By **Ashley Williams**

Trickin' On A Heaux For Christmas

Homie Hoppin' For The Holidays

Wet Dreams On Lockdown: The Female C.O

Letters Of His Love

By **Telia Teanna**

The State's Witness

The State's Witness 2

The State's Witness 3

This Time Won't You Save Me

This Time Won't You Save Me 2

His Summer Side Piece

A Holiday Heist

By **Kyiris Ashley**

Stuck In The Trenches

Stuck In The Trenches 2

By **Huff Tha Great**

Melted The Heart Of A Menace

Wet Dreams On Lockdown: Lieutenant Grace

By **P. Wise**

Merry Trapmas

By **Mia Sky**

Thug Me The Right Way

By **DiamondATL & Nai**

Wet Dreams On Lockdown: The Counselor

By **Paris Iman**

Wet Dreams On Lockdown: The Male C.O

By **Tamyra Griffin**

Wet Dreams On Lockdown: The Captain

By **TN Jones**

Wet Dreams On Lockdown: The Warden

By **Shawnice**

Atlantastan

Atlantastan 2

By **Chris Green**

IN The Streetz

IN The Streetz 2

IN The Streetz 3

By **Tron Hill**

Hittin' Licks For The Holidays: New York

By Freshh Moneyy

Coming Soon From
URBAN AINT DEAD

The Hottest Summer Ever 2
THE G-CODE
Tales 4rm Da Dale 2
How To Invest In The Stock Market From Prison
By **Elijah R. Freeman**

Hittaz 6
By **Lou Garden Price, Sr.**

Good Girls Gone Rogue 3
By **Manny Black**

Despite The Odds 2
By **Juhnell Morgan**

Charge It To The Game 3
By **Nai**

This Time Won't You Save Me 3
Healing The Heart Of A Detroit Gangsta
By **Kyiris Ashley**

Atlantastan 3
By **Chris Green**

IN The Streetz 5
By **Tron Hill**

BOOKS BY

URBAN AINT DEAD's C.E.O

<u>Elijah R. Freeman</u>

Triggadale 1, 2 & 3

Tales 4rm Da Dale

The Hottest Summer Ever

Murda Was The Case 1, 2 & 3

Hittin' Licks For The Holidays: Atlanta

Wet Dreams On Lockdown: The Nurse

How To Publish A Book From Prison

STAY CONNECTED

Follow
Elijah R. Freeman
On Social Media
FB: Elijah R. Freeman
IG: @the_future_of_urban_fiction